In a way, it wasn't such a bad life. Keefler could bring in his prisoners—the ones he especially hated—maimed or sometimes even dead, and the department would give him a reprimand and maybe suspend him for 60 days.

Then he could start in all over again.

Now that he'd caught Terry Judson in a parole violation and got him sent back to the can, Keefler felt he deserved a reward, so he went over to drop in on Judson's wife, Connie. She was a hefty, healthy redhead, and the re-arrest of her husband had taken all the steam out of her.

And, after all, was it Keefler's fault if Connie somehow got the idea that Keefler could get Judson sprung again? She was willing to put out. There wasn't a hell of a lot of life in her, but how much choice did a one-handed guy have?

Besides, it was a very nice thing to be able to lie there with her and think about how you put her husband back in jail. . . .

JOHN D. MacDONALD

THE PRICE OF MURDER

A FAWCETT GOLD MEDAL BOOK

Fawcett Publications, Inc., Greenwich, Conn.

THE PRICE OF MURDER

PROLOGUE

"If I could have the attention of the other members of the Commission for a moment, please. Let me reconstruct for you the actual physical details of the first murder.

"He was roughly ten feet from her. We know she turned and snatched upon the knife drawer. But he was on her before she could grasp one of the knives. He held her with his right hand at the nape of her neck. We are not certain of the position of his left arm. It may have been around her waist, but more probably, he grasped the rear of her . . . ah . . . garment in the vicinity of the waist. Then, gentlemen, he lifted her bodily and, with terrible force, brought her face and head down against the edge of the sink.

"I present three cranial X-rays and two photographs of the body which show the extent of the damage inflicted. By a careful examination of the fractures and other facial damage we can be certain that he lifted her and slammed her down no less than fifteen times, and it could possibly have been twice that. After the first impact she was certainly unconscious, perhaps dying. She presented a dead weight then of one hundred and fifteen pounds. Assuming a two-second cycle for each impact, he spent a full minute blindly smashing that lifeless body against the edge of the sink. Is that not the action of a sick mind?

"I now ask for a full minute of silence. During this minute please try to visualize that scene of murder. Go!"

CHAPTER ONE

Lee Bronson

The parole officer came to the house on a hot Saturday afternoon in October. Lee Bronson had set up a card table on the small screened porch of his rented house at 1024 Arcadia Street, where he sat reading and marking the English themes turned in on Friday by his English Composition 2A class of forty-one students at Brookton Junior College.

He sat in a wicker chair and wore a T-shirt with a torn shoulder, faded khakis, and old tennis shoes. The porch was on the front of the house, with a heavy screen of plantings that nearly concealed it from the pedestrians on the walk beyond the shallow front yard. Big elms grew on Arcadia Street, and their roots had buckled and cracked the old sidewalk. High branches touched over the middle of the street, and in the summer the dense shade lay heavily on the shallow front lawns of the frame houses.

When he looked up from his work he could see a segment of sidewalk and street. He could hear the sounds of the street. Motors of delivery trucks, whirring clack of roller skates, the nasal sputter of a small, familiar, and excessively noisy power mower several houses down on the other side of the street.

He was twenty-nine, a big man with wide hard shoulders, sculptured chest, wide bands of muscle linking neck and shoulders—narrow through waist and flank. He held himself trimly and moved lightly and with a quickness. His hair was brown and cut short, his eyes gray, quiet, slightly myopic. Though his face was bony, forthright, his habitual expression was one of mild patience, tinged by sadness, and when he was amused there was a wryness in the way his mouth turned down at the corners. With his black-

9

framed reading glasses on he looked properly scholarly. This was his third year at Brookton. His contract called for instruction in English and Physical Education. He acted as an assistant coach in the school athletic program, and worked at it hard enough to keep himself in trim.

He liked working with the kids. It gave him a sense of purpose. He liked to watch them grow and change, and feel that he had something to do with that growth. Yet it was only during his rare moods of complete depression that he was willing to admit to himself that without this joy in his work, his life would be unendurable. During those times he could clearly see the dimensions of the trap into which he had so blindly wandered. A perfumed trap. A silky and membranous and pneumatic little trap. A trap named Lucille.

He picked up the next composition. This was a new class. He had just begun to associate faces with the names. Jill Grossman. A strange and terrified little mouse, almost an albino, with a pinched little face and glasses with a blue tint. But her work had talent. He decided he would like to ask her to join his unofficial seminar, the kids he invited over to the house in the evenings.

But Lucille was being even more difficult about such get-togethers this year than last. She could not see any reason for doing anything you were not paid to do. Lucille flounced off to the movies on those evenings.

After he had marked Jill's paper, and made marginal notes cautioning her about being too florid and precious, he looked at his watch. A little after four. He hoped Lucille would remember to bring back the cold six-pack of beer he'd asked for. But it wasn't likely. But he was certain of one thing she would bring back—her standard comments about how grim it was to have to use the public pool to go swim with Ruthie, her best girl friend, when, if they could belong to Crown Ridge Club which was so cheap really, and they could get in easy, the pool was really lovely with lights under the water at night, and she could take Ruthie there, and all winter they had the dances. And of course they didn't belong to the Crown Ridge Club because he didn't love her. It was the only possible answer. He was taking her for granted. It was

10

impossible to explain family finances to Lucille. Figures bored her.

And any serious attempt to make her understand the budget always gave her a new opening.

"So if we're so poor we can't join just one cheap little club, why don't you write another book and make some money? You wrote a book, didn't you? So you could write for the television and the movies and the big magazines, couldn't you? Instead of having those weird kids coming over here all the time, you could be writing and making some money so we could live nicer. You don't *want* me to have nice things. That's it, isn't it? You just don't *care* any more."

And it was useless to try to explain to her that his single book had used up a whole year of creative energy, that it had earned a big two hundred and fifty dollar advance and a magnificent one hundred and eighteen dollars and thirty-three cents in additional royalties. No use to try to tell her that his talent was small, and that it certainly could not accomplish anything in the environment she had helped create. The kids were his creative outlet. But he had displayed the "author" tag far too prominently during their brief courtship. It gave her a weapon she could never resist wielding.

Just as he picked up the final composition in the pile he had brought home, somebody banged on the screen door, banged with unnecessary loudness, with a flavor of irritation and arrogance. From where Lee sat he could see baggy knees of gray pants, a slice of white shirt.

He pushed his chair back and started to get up. The screen door was pulled open and a man walked in. He was a thickset man, heavy around the middle, with a lean hollow-cheeked face that did not match his puffy build. A tan felt hat with a sweat-stained band was pushed back off his forehead. His nose was bulbous at the tip, and patterned with small broken red veins, prominent against the uniform pallid gray of his face. His eyes were small and blue and the flesh around them was dark-stained and puffy. He carried his gray suit coat over his left arm. The left hand, in a soiled white glove that fit too tightly, was

11

obviously artificial. His hard black shoes were dusty and he walked toward Lee as though his feet were tender.

He could have been an aggressive and seldom success-ful door to door salesman. Or the man who always stands in the neighborhood bar, propounding noxious and illogi-cal argument. But the warning bells of Lee's childhood were still efficient. He concealed his irritation and said evenly, "Is there something I can do for you?"

"Bronson?" Lee nodded. The man took out a wallet, flipped it open and held it out. "Keefler. Parole officer."

He sat in the other wicker chair without invitation, sighed, shoved his hat back another half inch and said, "Every day they say relief in sight. Last heat wave of the year will end. It gets hotter."

"Is this about Dan?"

Keefler looked at him with a hard, lazy tolerance that had an undertone of cynical amusement. "So who else? Is there more than one ex-con in the family? Maybe I'm missing something."

"I thought a man named Richardson was . . ."

"Rich used to have him. Now he's mine. It's like this, Bronson. I was a cop up to four months ago when they took off my hand. A young punk snuck his brother's army .45 out of the house and tried to stick up a market, and lucky Keefler came along and took one right in the wrist and got it smashed too bad to save. Maybe you read about it."

"I think I remember it. You killed the boy, didn't you?"

"And I got a citation and a new job with the parole people and a dummy hand. Because I was a cop they've given me the rough cases. So now I've got your brother Danny. When was the last time you saw him?"

"I'll have to think back, Mr. Keefler. He came here after he was paroled. That was last May. And I think two other times. The last time was in July. I can tell you the exact date. The twenty-fifth."

"How come you happen to remember the exact day?"

"I remember it because it was the day after my birth-day. He brought me a present."

"What kind of a present? Expensive?"

12

"A leather desk set with pen and pencil and clock calendar."

"Let's have a look at it."

"It's at school, in my office."

"What do you think it would cost?"

"About thirty dollars, I'd guess."

"What did he have to say about how he was doing?"

"He didn't say much. Maybe I could be more help to you if you'd tell me what you're after."

Keefler plucked a cigarette from his shirt pocket, bent a match over in a folder of book matches and lit it with one hand. "Like that? Nurse in the hospital showed me how you do it."

"Pretty good."

"I can hold matches in this artificial hand. See? But its slower. Let's get back to Danny. You'd cover for him, wouldn't you?"

Lee looked at Bronson's lazy, wise half smile. "Would it make any difference how I answered that?"

"It might."

"I can't prove I wouldn't. I might run into a situation where I would. But I wouldn't put myself in the bag, Mr. Keefler, unless there was a good reason. You've talked to Mr. Richardson."

"He filled me in. He likes those big words. All the social workers know those big words. You and Danny and I all came from the Sink. We know the rules down there. We don't need the big social worker words, do we?"

The Sink was the name given to thirty city blocks in Hancock. Long ago Brookton had been a separate community, a farming community outside Hancock. But the big sprawl of the lake-side city had reached out and surrounded Brookton. The Sink was the oldest part of Hancock, built when Hancock had been a small, lusty, violent lake port. The derivation of the name had been forgotten. The thirty blocks were down in the flats between the old docks and warehouses and the railroad yards. It had always been the spawning bed for Hancock's impressive output of criminals. Slum clearance projects had removed all but a narrow fringe of the original Sink.

"It wasn't an easy place to grow up," Lee said.

13

Keefler nodded. "There was just the two of you, wasn't there?"

"Danny and me. He's three years older. My father was half owner of a tug. He died before I was a year old."

Keefler grinned. "He was dead drunk and he fell between the dock and an ore freighter. He was thirty-nine and your mother was twenty-three at the time. Her maiden name was Elvita Sharon and her folks ran a hunting lodge in northern Wisconsin and your father met her there on a hunting trip and ran off with her. After Jerry Bronson died, she married Rudy Fernandez. Bronson hadn't left her a dime. Rudy was a dock worker. He was a trouble maker. A little while after they were married, Rudy was beat half to death. That's when you moved into the Sink. When he got back on his feet, and tried to make more trouble, they killed him. It's still on the books. Then she hooked up with a slob named Cowley, and there isn't any record of any marriage on the books. When you were twelve and Danny was fifteen, Cowley died of a heart attack. The three of you lived in a cold-water flat at 1214 River Street, on the third floor. Elvita was a part-time waitress and a full-time lush. Both you kids were bringing money home, just enough so you could keep going."

Lee looked down at his right hand and closed it slowly into a fist. "You seem to have the whole story, Keefler."

"Right out of those social worker files, boy. They have to know why a guy like Danny can't . . . adjust to reality. But it seemed pretty real down there, didn't it? Danny quit school at sixteen and went to work for Nick Bouchard. By the time he was nineteen he was bringing enough home so Elvita didn't have to work at all. I was watching him then. He was a wise punk. I could have told all the social workers how he'd come out."

"He was the oldest. He thought he had to . . ."

"He went where the fast money was. Right to Nick, the big boss man." Keefler chuckled. "Nick took good care of the Bronson boys."

"Not me. I wasn't any part of it."

Keefler's eyes went round with surprise. "No? You were being the hotshot highschool athlete. I thought that when

14

Danny took his first fall, that two and a half years he did for auto theft, Nick sent money to you every week."

"He did. But it wasn't like that. It was part of the agreement he had with Danny. It had nothing to do with me. I talked to Nick. He . . . he wanted me to get out of the Sink."

"He helped you out of some trouble, didn't he? You're on the books, boy. Assault. And the charge was dismissed, and it was Nick's lawyers who took care of you."

"There wasn't any assault, Mr. Keefler. I was working in a wholesale grocery warehouse nights. I got picked up when I was walking home. I'd barked my knuckles on a packing case. They were looking for some men who'd broken up a bar and grill."

"Now that sounds reasonable," Keefler said softly.

Lee looked sharply at him. Keefler looked sleepy and contented and amiable.

"Nick Bouchard wasn't all bad," Lee said.

"Hell, no. He helped you go through college, didn't he? So he couldn't be such a bad guy."

"The way you say it, it doesn't sound right, Mr. Keefler. I had a football scholarship. Danny used to send me money. Nick used to send some too, a twenty or a fifty, with a note telling me to live it up. I guess I was . . . a hobby with Nick. I played good ball the first two years. Then after my eyes went bad and they shifted me to guard, my leg went bad."

"You say I put things the wrong way. So tell me what happened to your mother. Tell it your way."

"Is it important?"

"Come on, boy. Put it in your words. You've got the education."

"It . . . happened in my sophomore year. In December. Danny had moved her out of the Sink the previous spring. She . . . went back to the Sink to look up old friends. It was a cold night. She started drinking and she passed out in an alley, and by the time she was found it was too late. I came back for the funeral."

Keefler nodded. "That's just about the way it looks on the records, kid. And then the next year Nick got too big for his pants and tried to fight the syndicate so they cut him down and made it look like suicide, and a man named Kennedy came in and took over the boss job. He figured Danny had been too loyal to Nick, so Danny took his second fall."

"For something he didn't do."

"He just got elected for it. Think of the things he did do, kid." Keefler dropped his cigarette on the porch floor and rubbed it out with the sole of a black shoe. "Both the Bronson boys would have made out better if Nick had been smart enough to stay in the saddle."

"I don't see how it made any difference to me."

"Oh, sure. He wanted to help you get out of the Sink. Until you got a college education."

"It hurt Danny. I'll admit that. But when I graduated, I wasn't a football bum looking for a job with Nick or anybody like him. I graduated with good marks."

"I know, I know," Keefler said wearily. "And you got yourself wounded and decorated in Korea and you came back and went to Columbia Graduate School on the G.I. Bill. I'm talking about what you *would* have done."

But Lee knew he had done what seemed inevitable. After hospital time in Japan, he was sent back on a hospital ship, was completely ambulatory by the time they docked at San Francisco. His request for discharge at Dix was granted. He enrolled in Columbia Graduate School, carried the heaviest work load they would give him, and earned his Master's.

By then he had destroyed the short stories and the notes for the novel. He had over seventy pages done on an entirely different novel. He had three hundred dollars. The placement agency had come up with the instructorship at Brookton Junior College. He went out for an interview and signed a contract. During that summer he worked on a road job to get back in shape. After the first week of exhaustion he began to adjust to the labor, and began work again on the book. The construction company was working on a stretch of new divided highway in southern Michigan where rooms were hard to find. He found a room in the farmhouse of a couple named Detterich. They had three young sons on the farm and an older daughter working in an insurance office in Battle Creek.

The daughter came home to the farm for her vacation—the last two weeks of August. Her name was Lucille. She was the loveliest thing he had ever seen.

The following December, after half a dozen trips in the ancient Plymouth he had purchased in order to be able to drive down to Battle Creek, and after he had been with his new job long enough to know that he liked it and could do it well, and after he had received the advance on his book of two hundred and fifty dollars, he married her in the parlor of the Detterich farmhouse on the second day of the Christmas vacation. They honeymooned in New Orleans, an unexpected honeymoon made possible by Danny's wedding gift of five crackling new hundred dollar bills, wrapped in a sheet of hotel stationery on which he had scrawled, *Have a ball, kids.* Danny had been out for a year and a half. He was back in Hancock, and he seemed to be doing very well indeed.

Lee Bronson was twenty-six. He had work he liked. The pay was low, but the acceptance of the book took the sting out of that. There would be more books, and there would come a day when he could either go on teaching or give it up, as he chose. He had a bride men turned in the street to stare at. The world was a fine place, that December.

Danny lost again the following March, the same month they found the house on Arcadia Street and moved out of the dingy furnished apartment. Lee went down to see him, before he was sentenced. Danny was a little heavier. He was a week away from being thirty. He was very depressed, and he marveled bitterly at his bad fortune.

"Twice before I got picked up, Lee, and neither damn time had I done what I got sent up for. This time it's worse, almost. Now, get this: I'm way uptown, at Sonny's. I'm at the bar, a little loaded, but minding my own business. It's four in the afternoon. Day before yesterday. I got a date in the bar. She's coming in to meet me at five. The bar is empty except for a couple down the bar. They're having a fight. I'm paying no attention. I'm just there drinking my drink, damn it. The woman isn't bad looking, not bad at all. They're both drinking and barking at each other. All of a sudden she comes down, takes the

17

stool next to me, grabs my arm and says I should buy her a drink. It's nothing to me. So I do. You know that's a nice place. A good trade. No trouble. He comes down. She won't look at him or talk to him. He's a big joker. My size. Maybe fifteen years older. He starts grabbing at her. Rough like. I tell him to take it easy. The bartender tells him. But no. The big shot has to grab me by the shoulder, spin me around and swing. I ducked my head and he hit me right on top of the head. It hurt. I was drinking. I wasn't so lucky it left a mark where he hit. It's still a little sore, but no mark. Enough is enough. I rush him right back into a corner, fast. Wham, wham, wham. Maybe I hit him four five times, every one right down the alley. I had to hold him up for the last one. Nothing dirty. No knee. Nothing. Like a gentleman I did it, every one on the mouth and he bleeds all over the place. I let him drop, got my hat off the stool next to mine and left a buck tip out of my change and took off. They don't know me so good there. But you see, I got this date I got to come back for. I come back and I'm grabbed. I think it's like a joke. No joke, kid. Assault. The big guy's name is Fitch. He's big news. A banker from Detroit and he stops there when he's in town. The bitch he was fighting with is his wife. He once upon a time loaned Sonny some money, I hear. So it goes down like this, and this is what the three of them say, the only witnesses. I come in loaded. I make a pass at his wife. He objects. The bartender tells me to leave. So I beat up on the banker and walk out. Busted his jaw, not too bad, and ruined a lot of expensive dentist work. I give Kennedy the picture. No dice. It's too hot. Maybe I'm not worth the trouble. So here I go again. Jesus, Lee!"

And he went again. He was given a one to ten, that curious sentence that means a man is eligible for parole after one year but, in the discretion of the warden and the parole board, can be kept for the full ten.

Daniel Bronson served two and a half years, less one month. He came to see Lee when he was released. He was a silent and sour man. He had found a job, prior to release, with a trucking firm, the owner of which, having done time in his youth, was willing to hire ex-convicts and

18

men on parole. Lee had asked him if it was a blind, a myth for the parole people as other jobs had been the other times he had been released.

"No. I've been a sucker long enough, kid."

"Going straight?"

Danny's smile was slow and savage. "This late? I've lived very well. I can't adjust at this late date to a beer and beans existence."

Lee remembered his surprise at the choice of words and the careful diction, and he remembered that Danny noticed his surprise. Still smiling, he had said, "Don't be a snob, little brother. I've always been smart enough, I think. I learned to handle myself right, and I learned to wear the right clothes. I was fine until I opened my stupid mouth. So this time I didn't waste my time up there in Altuu. I haven't got your fancy degrees, kid, but from now on it's going to be harder for people to figure me out. I finished high school English requirements. I read books, kid. Maybe a hundred books."

"I still don't know what you have in mind."

"Neither do I. Yet. But I'm not going to play horse for Kennedy. Sooner or later I'd take the fourth fall and get tagged an habitual. Seven and a half years out of thirty-two on the inside. I'm going to find an angle, sooner or later. I'm going to look and I'm going to find one, and until I do I'll wheel a rig for Grunwalt, draw my pay, and tell Kennedy to shove it if he tries to hook me back in. The organization never gave me anything but a bad time. I want a solo kick."

That had been in May. The next time he had stopped by had been in June, and he was still working for Grunwalt. But the last time Lee had seen him, in late July, Danny's situation had obviously changed. He had been driving a late model sedan, a medium-priced car, gray and inconspicuous. He had been wearing a rayon cord suit, a narrow maroon knit tie, a button-down collar. Lee had just come back from teaching a summer session class when Danny had come striding up the walk, gift-wrapped box under his arm. He had thought at the time that if you didn't know Danny's history you could easily take him for a successful youngish man of the salesman type. He was a bit shorter than Lee, and broader, with heavier bones. His hair, paler than Lee's, was a dark blond, with a tight kinky wave.

Up close, the illusion suffered. There were the small scars, and the bright, cold, predatory eyes, and the restless, reckless flavor of all the bad ones. Lee, worried about what he might be up to, had tried to question him. Though Danny fended off the questions with smiling ease, Lee caught an impression that surprised him. Whatever Danny was doing, he was slightly shamefaced about it, as though it did not fit his own picture of himself.

And whatever Danny was doing—it had brought Keefler here on this hot afternoon. Keefler seemed sleepy and reasonable. But too anxious to lump Lee with Danny.

"Look, Mr. Keefler. Danny went in the wrong direction. He started early. Maybe it's too late for anything to be done. I don't know. But I didn't go in that direction, and you didn't go in that direction. We got out of the Sink."

Keefler raised one eyebrow. "We?"

"You and me, Mr. Keefler."

"Let me get this." He pointed at Lee's chest and then his own. "You want to put us in the same bundle. But it doesn't work that way."

"Why not?"

"Because I come up by myself. You got your way bought for you. With stinking money from a hood brother and stinking money from a big mobster. You want to lump yourself with somebody, you fit with Danny, not with me."

In the moment of shock before anger came, Lee felt astonished at the sudden bitterness and the unreasoning anger of the man. When Lee's anger was complete, he did not let it change his voice or his expression. "I was under the ridiculous impression that we were reminiscing, Mr. Keefler. You are sitting on my porch in a chair I bought, dropping ashes on a porch I painted. You are a parole officer. I am an instructor at a state educational institution. I've tried to be pleasant to you for Danny's sake. If you have questions, ask them. But from now on, watch your mouth and your manners."

20

Keefler stared at him for long seconds. Then he chuckled and said, "Now if you aren't the one!"

"Ask your questions."

"Sure, but first I'll make *my* little speech. They keep telling me it's a free country. It don't mean a thing to me if you wave your education in my face. Not a thing. There's a fence, see? Right across the middle of the world. I'm on one side. And the Bronson boys are on the other. You both got records. You're both in the files. He's got a thicker file. I'll talk to you just the same way I talk to anybody on the other side of that fence. I got a right to talk to anybody I want to. And you are going to play it my way. If you don't like my way, and if I think maybe you're hiding something, I go over to that school you work at, and I got my hat in my hand and I ask them a hell of a lot of polite questions about you, and if when I'm through there's anybody left over there that doesn't know you got a brother who's a three-time loser who put you through school on stolen money, it's going to surprise both of us. And they'll know your brother has busted his parole and he's on the loose and he gives you fancy presents. And they'll know you got picked up on an assault charge and it got squashed because the guy who showed up to squash it was the smart shyster who worked for Nick Bouchard. If they still love you over there, I'll see you get pulled in for questioning, and I'll see it happens often, and I'll make sure it comes when you should be teaching like they are paying you for. Now if you think they'll still keep paying you for teaching after all that, you can pop off some more about my mouth and my manners. To Johnny Keefler, you are one of the Bronson boys, and both the Bronson boys stink. End of speech."

Anger had suddenly become much too expensive. A luxury. He straightened the papers on the card table and he was annoyed with himself to see that his hand was shaking. He saw the factor he had missed in Keefler's personality. The man was not entirely sane. He was perfectly capable of doing exactly what he threatened. He would do it knowing well that he would gain nothing but the satisfaction of smashing the orderly life of Lee Bronson. Perhaps, before the loss of the hand, he had been

21

merely a tough cop with a streak of sadism. Lee knew he had no important contacts, no place he could go and ask that Keefler be pulled off him. He knew that the only thing he could do was crawl. And it was humiliating even with the rationalization that it was but to placate a madman.

He looked down at the stack of themes, and spoke in an expressionless voice. "He came here on the afternoon of July twenty-fifth. He was too well dressed to be still working for Grunwalt. He was driving a gray two-door, a recent model. Maybe a Dodge or a Plymouth. He stayed from about three-thirty to five-thirty. We had some drinks. I wondered what he was doing. He wouldn't tell me. He admitted he wasn't at Grunwalt's. I asked if Rich knew about that. He said it was all fixed. I asked him if he'd gone back with Kennedy and he said no."

"Now you're being a good boy, but it's a lot of crap you're handing me. He's your brother. If he was onto something, he'd tell you."

"I can only give you my word that he didn't. My wife was with us all the time. She'll tell you the same thing."

"Where's your wife?"

"She's due back any minute. In fact, she's a little late."

"I got the time."

"Don't lean on her, Mr. Keefler. She's not used to . . ."

"You forget easy. I'm doing this my way, Bronson. Where is Danny now?"

"I haven't any idea."

"You act like you *want* to make it hard for yourself. We'll get him anyway. He broke parole. So he owes the state seven years and seven months. There's no way in the world he can get out of that."

"I'll tell you one thing. It doesn't sound right. It doesn't sound like him. He's smarter than that."

Keefler gave a snort of contempt. "That clown isn't smart. No three-time loser has brains, professor. Here's how smart I am. Rich and those other guys were carrying too big a load. So they're told to turn over so many files apiece to me, and make it the rough ones. From Rich I get your brother and a few others. He briefs me on them. They're all doing fine, he says. Danny Bronson is checking in like he should. No trouble with Danny. No trouble

22

at all. He gives me the big words. Fine adjustment. Social conscience. Crap! I ask when he's due in, and Rich says he phones in. I ask if he ever stops over to see him on the job and Rich says it might embarrass the men to go drop in on them. First I go check on where he's living. I find he moved out of that flea bag room early in July. There's a violation right there. Change of address without notification or authorization. No forwarding address. Then I go to Grunwalt. Bronson, sure. Worked here for six weeks. Quit the end of June. As far as Rich knew, he was still working there. So he's a wise guy, and I've decided he's had too much fresh air and he's due back inside to think it over. So I drift around town, asking who's seen him. Nobody. While I'm looking he phones Rich on schedule, a local call. By then I've told Rich off, told him how the wise punk was kidding him. Maybe over the phone Rich breaks into tears or something, telling the poor fella how he's let his friends down. That call came in last Monday. I'm still looking. He's on the tape now, with a pick-up order out for him. I got the rest of my punks hacked into line. They jump up and say sir. Rich and those other clowns are too soft. I'm going to get Danny and he's going to go down on his knees and he's going to beg and he's going to blubber, and then he's going back to Alton for violation of parole, and by God, he's going to stay there. Your smart brother wasn't a damn bit smart, Bronson."

"All I can tell you is I honestly don't know where he is, Keefler."

"*Mister* Keefler."

"Mister Keefler."

"Try it again, with a little more snap, professor."

"*Mister* Keefler."

"That's better. You saw him last on the twenty-fifth of July?"

"That's right."

"Try it again, with a sir."

"That's right, sir."

"You're coming along nice, professor. You're certain you haven't seen him since?"

"I'm positive . . . sir."

23

"What are all those papers, Bronson?"

"Class work, sir. English themes."

Keefler stood up, reached over and took the top paper. Jill Grossman's work. He read it, frowning, his lips moving, for about twenty seconds. Then he tossed it contemptuously on the desk. "Good god, is that what you teach them? What the hell is it about?"

"I wouldn't expect you to understand."

"Different people don't understand different things. Think the parents of those kids would understand about you? About your old lady, maybe? The record says she was a lush, a part-time waitress and a part-time whore that got herself froze to death in an alley in the Sink."

Lee's hand was on his knee, hidden by the table top. He looked up at Keefler's smile and, keeping his face blank, he closed his hand into a hard fist. He could hear the sound it would make against that slack smile, and he could feel how it would jolt all the way up to his shoulder. He had the feeling that Keefler knew exactly what was coming, and had known just how to push him over the edge. But at that crucial moment he heard the muted yelp of tires and the bang of springs and shocks as Lucille drove the old Plymouth into their driveway in her normal frantic fashion.

"This your wife now?" Keefler asked. Lee nodded, not quite trusting himself to speak. Keefler sat down. Lee felt weak and sick with reaction. Keefler said, "You stay put, professor. She'll come on out here by herself, won't she?"

"Yes. She'll come out here."

"What else? Come on, get it up."

"Sir."

He heard Lucille coming through the house, heard the clack of her clogs on the hardwood in the hallway, the softer sound of her steps on the rug. She came out onto the porch, saying, in a whining voice, "Honey, you just gotta do something about the car. When I stopped to let Ruthie off, it stalled and I . . ." She stopped as she saw Keefler. Lee saw her quick and expert appraisal of him, saw her arrive at the immediate conclusion that Keefler could be of no interest to her, saw her face change into

24

the look of hauteur and indifference she reserved for everybody she considered the least bit inferior.

"Lucille, this is Mr. Keefler. He's Danny's parole officer."

And the look of indifference was gone, and Lee saw a curious alertness about her. "How do you do," she said, very politely.

"Hi, Lucille," Keefler said, remaining stolidly in his chair. Lee had screened the porch a year and a half ago, and he had left the original railings. The screen was about eight inches beyond the railing. Lucille moved over and sat on the railing, long round legs straight, crossed at the ankles. She wore her dark blue swim suit, a short pale blue beach coat of thick terrycloth over it, and wooden clogs with white straps. Her hands were shoved deeply into the big pockets of the short beach coat, and the collar was turned up. Her hair was the coppery dark of old pennies, and coiled tightly, the coils no larger than coins, hair fitting her head closely with a look of spirit and bravery like a Roman youth. She was, Lee thought, almost unchanged by three years of marriage. Her perfect face had babyish blandness, large blue eyes set very wide, elfin snub of a nose, lips wide and heavy, teeth a bit too small and of a perfect white. She was now, as she had been three years before, one of the most provocative looking women he had ever seen. The life of her seemed so very close to the sensitive and unflawed satin of her skin. It was visibly warm in the pulse of her throat, in the lucent blue of veins at temple, wrist and ankle. Her long legs seemed to have extra curvatures, tender hollows, velvety paddings which, in other women, were but the hints of what here, in her, was almost too graphically expressed.

She usually kept her hands out of sight. They were small hands, but thick through the palms, with very short fingers. The nails were deeply nibbled and ugly.

Now she had her perfect summer tan, a honeyed luminescence that seemed more a glow of gold from beneath the skin than a deepening of color of the skin itself. The whites of her eyes were blued with her perfect health. There had been a little change. Her waist did not nip in above the sweet abundance of hips with quite such a

25

startling contrast; there was a tiny roll of fat around her middle. There was a fullness under her chin, a small pad that unfortunately made it slightly apparent that there was not a great deal of chin in the first place. Her round high breasts were larger, the tissues less firm. And there were two tiny brackets of discontent around her mouth.

He remembered a time last May when she had been at the school to meet him and had somehow missed him, and he had been hurrying to catch up with her when he spotted her a half block ahead, walking toward home, walking with her short quick steps, hips swinging in wine linen slacks. As he had come up behind two boys who were following her, keeping pace with her, he heard one of them say, with thick-throated fervor, "Damn! She's really built for it."

That phrase had remained in his mind because it had been, in a curious way, an index of his self-betrayal. In the very beginning she had been the perfect delusion. Blinded by that magical face and body, he had read into her all the things he wanted to find. Her wide-eyed look was honesty. Her farm background and the office job in Battle Creek denoted energy and integrity. He detected an undertone of seeming cleverness in her most banal remark. Her automatic sexual hunger could not be anything but love.

He could not believe that a face and body of such perfections could contain a third-class mind. He told himself that her environment had not given her a chance to grow. When he talked she looked at him with shining eyes and rapt attention that could only come from a superior intelligence and from a sensitivity that had never been given a chance to develop. He would develop it. He would take delight in her growth.

He had been stubborn, and it had taken a year before he could see her clearly and know how poor had been the bargain he had struck. As the first child and only daughter of the Detterichs she had been grievously spoiled. She had been that rarity—a beautiful baby, a beautiful child, a beautiful adolescent. In a world where beauty was so highly prized, it was only necessary to be looked at and admired. She had learned that she was a great prize, and

26

that it was inevitable that she would be given all the good things of the world. By someone. Her parents gave all they could. She was never given chores. She never made her own bed, or cleaned her room. In school she had been an indifferent scholar, a bland dreamer without intellectual resource. In her dreams she was a famous actress, or singer, or movie star. But never was there any effort to implement these dreams.

Even the job, he learned, had been a phony. She had dropped out of high school in the middle of her junior year, and for the next two years had done absolutely nothing, rising at noon, washing her hair, lounging around the farmhouse, waiting only for dusk and the inevitable car in the drive, the peremptory honk, the long evening date. Boredom had finally driven her to Battle Creek. After a six weeks' course at a business school, during which she had learned very little, she had gone to work for her uncle, her mother's brother, a general agent. Lee remembered the way Uncle Rog had said, "Seel dressed up the office pretty good." And chuckled. "Hard to keep the boys out working on prospects. Used to be if you wanted to lose anything for good, have Seel file it."

The last illusion to go was the one of love. Unlike the norm of most beautiful women, she was strongly, hungrily sexed. But her only interest was her own gratification. He existed as an available instrument of her completion, not as a person. She would say the expected words of love, but as a short lesson learned by rote.

He knew that, as a person, he did not exist for her. Nor did anyone else in the world really exist. She lived entirely for herself, and anyone who entered her life in any way existed only as a part of the frame around her. Should they fit her preconceived notion of herself, they were acceptable. If they did not fit, they were ignored.

She was an indifferent housekeeper, a dull, lazy and unimaginative cook. In his final knowledge he admitted to himself that she was stupid, lazy, insensitive, greedy, superficial and curiously coarse. He had thought a child might change her, but after he became convinced they could not conceive, he felt a guilty relief. He took the joyless use of her that she took of him. And he intoned

27

the expected words with her own lack of conviction. He felt responsibility toward her. He did not feel that he could leave her. And when he thought of how she would be in twenty years, soft, fat, querulous, whining, his heart seemed to hang sick and heavy in his breast. He knew she would hurt him in his profession. At the moment it was not too important. At faculty affairs she was decorative, and when she opened her mouth and the emptinesses came out, it was thought cute. Lucille, the doll-wife.

The one factor he most resented was the way she managed to stifle his ability to do a second novel. He tried. He could not work. There was always the knowledge of her in the house. Her listless boredom, her sighing discontent. She felt he had cheated her somehow. This life was too meager. She didn't understand money, or how to handle it. She merely knew that she had to have a great deal more than she had. Her desires were infantile. She wanted a glossy convertible, country club membership, a mink, travel, matched luggage, a fulltime maid, and one really good square-cut emerald. Lee obviously couldn't acquire those things and never would. So Lee had cheated her. And her family felt Lee had cheated her.

As he was unable to work at what he wanted most to do, he had filled his time as completely as he could with extra work. Any obligation was preferable to the endless evenings after eating one of those frozen horrors she purchased called "television dinners," trying to read in the small living room while she lived the spurious life of the picture tube.

The marriage had become a curious armed truce. In a small and very guilty corner of his soul he hoped that out of her ignorance and her boredom she would commit some act so monstrous that it would cancel his obligation to her and he would be free of her. Though he had the dark suspicion that there had been very few personable men in her home neighborhood who had not managed to trigger her quick physical responses, she seemed now to be utterly faithful. She spent a great deal of time with Ruthie Loftis, the plump brunette wife of a car salesman who lived three blocks down Arcadia Street. Ruthie was cut from the same pattern. When he was forced to over-

28

hear fifteen minutes of any Lucille-Ruthie conversation, he felt like throwing his head back and roaring like a gut-shot bear.

He glanced at Keefler and saw that the man was looking at Lucille with cold avidity and an overtone of astonishment.

"Seems like your brother-in-law Danny has come up missing," Keefler said easily. "When was the the last time you saw him? Now don't look at him, honey. You look at me and tell me."

"Gee, I got to think. It was a *long* time ago. Lee, wasn't it about your birthday?"

"I told you not to look at him."

"I'm sorry. It's like a game, sort of, huh? He was here the day after Lee's birthday, when he was twenty-nine I'm twenty-four. Let me see. He brought you something. I can't remem . . . oh, that stuff for your desk. I don't know why he had to bring junk like that."

"Have you seen him since?"

Lucille's eyes looked wider. She shook her head from side to side, with the slow solemnity of a child. "No, Mr. Keefler. We haven't seen him at all."

Lee felt the tension at the nape of his neck. Lucille was a congenital liar, and a poor one. There were always reasons for her lies. Where did the change go? Gee, honey, it must have fallen out of my pocket. Those are new shoes, aren't they? Are you crazy! I've had these for ages. Why didn't you tell me Dr. Ewing called? But he didn't, honest. Always with the same extra width of eye, the same slow shake of her lovely head, the slight abused pout of her heavy lips. He had seen it so many times that he knew beyond any doubt that Lucille was lying to Keefler. He looked narrowly at Keefler, who took out a cigarette and lit the match one-handed. Keefler stood up. "Well, you back up what your husband told me, Mrs. Bronson. I guess you folks are in the clear."

He started toward the screen door and turned sharply and said, "What work is he doing, Lucille? What work is Danny doing?"

"Gee, I don't know. Honest. He wouldn't say."

Keefler stood by the screen door, nibbling his lower lip. "Go on in the house, honey," he said.

Lee saw Lucille obey with an unexpected docility. She never took readily to being ordered about. Keefler gestured to Lee. He got up and walked over. Keefler looked up at him. "Big bastard, aren't you?"

"Is that a question . . . sir?"

"Don't get porky. You can't afford it. You don't mean anything to me. I can step on you like on a bug. Now I'm telling you just what you're going to do. You're going to wait, and if you get any kind of word from Danny, you aren't going to wait ten seconds before you get hold of me. You're going to move fast, Bronson. Because if you don't, you're going to be the sorriest guy in the state. Right now he's a wanted man. Understand? You hide one single damn thing, and there's laws that cover that, and I'll go to a lot of work to see that I make them stick."

Keefler settled his hat more squarely on his head. He shook out his suit coat and rehung it over his left arm. He went down the steps and out to the walk. He looked back once and lifted his arm in a sardonic gesture of farewell.

CHAPTER TWO

Johnny Keefler

When Keefler looked back the second time, Bronson was no longer standing behind the screen door. There were four blocks to walk, and even though it was five o'clock, it was still a thick hot day. He felt satisfaction when he thought of Lee Bronson. A punk like his brother, Hilda behind that big education, but still a punk. Two kinds of people. The ones with a record and the ones without. Traffic arrests were the only kind you couldn't count. The rest of them all had larceny in their hearts. Give Lee Bronson the right chance and he'd make a grab, same as the rest of them.

There was an alley in the back of Keefler's mind. It had been there the day it happened, and it would be there all the days of his life. A squalid alley in the Sink, a narrow path between the knee-deep litter that lay against the walls of the buildings on either side. No window looked down into that alley.

After his father had died, he and the two younger ones had been in the Home for over three years. Then his uncle took him out. His uncle, Mose Keefler, had run a small grocery store in the Sink and lived over it with his wife and his two daughters and the monster son they kept in the room in the back. Johnny Keefler had been nine when Mose got him out of the Home. Mose was a burly, somber, hardworking man and Johnny had adored him. The store was open from seven in the morning until eleven at night six days a week, noon to nine on Sundays. Mose drove himself, his wife, his daughters and Johnny hard. He scouted the farmers' market for half-spoiled merchandise that could be salvaged. Johnny could still remember the slime and the stink of rotten potatoes,

31

remember squatting in the shed behind the store, sorting good from bad. The store made just enough to support the six of them. For Johnny it was school and work and exhausted sleep on the army cot in the shed. He was a small spindly boy, subject to head colds, and with the tight, pinched, gray face of a slum diet.

Mose Keefler tried to maintain a fruit rack outside the store during the daylight hours. There was a bus stop at the corner and he picked up additional business that way. But he was in constant warfare with the roving band of tough kids who considered it their neighborhood. They would post a lookout across the street to signal when nobody was near the front of the store. Then the others would come on the run, snatching the pears, peaches, melons, apples, oranges. Johnny knew who they were. They went to the same school, the John X. Moran School on Hoffer Street. Red Annlie was the chieftain. And there was Gil Kowalsik, Hank Rillyer, Stubs Rollins, Tooey Gennetti, Pete Casey. They were all in the seventh and eighth grades at the school, even though Red was seventeen and big as a man. They made the lives of smaller kids a misery. They had casually tormented Johnny Keefler, but he was too small and cowed to provide much sport.

The police told Mose Keefler that if he could catch one of the kids, then maybe they could do something. Mose thought about it a long time and finally piled cartons just inside the door, made himself a peep-hole and hid behind it. On a Saturday afternoon there was a raid on the fruit. Mose came roaring out and, in two bounds, caught Hank Rillyer by the arm and started beating him around the head with his other hand. Johnny had run out, too. It was a day of misty rain. Hank was a wiry kid. Johnny saw the sleek gleam of the broad blade of the knife, gray as the sky, and yelled as he saw it sweep and cut. The knife had a razor edge. It cut across and through the stained apron, through the threadbare gray pants, through paunchy skin and the deep fat layers. It cut from side to side, an inch below the belt, a cut over a foot long. And Hank Rillyer ran, head down, thin legs pumping. Mose caught at himself with both hands, but he felt through his hands and looked down with wet ashen face at the gray and white and red, at the coils and clumps of his own substance. He went to his knees, still staring, and fell forward screaming in a voice that sounded far, far away. And died of shock on the operating table while they were rinsing the sidewalk filth from his organs.

Johnny Keefler, dry-eyed, feeling as far away as Mose's screams, told the police who did it, how it was done, and who was with the boy who did it. He had seen Rollins and Gennetti. They were picked up. They were sixteen and over. Rillyer got life for felony murder. Rollins and Gennetti were also tried. Gennetti got ten years. Rollins, whose father had good connections, got a suspended sentence. But long before they were sentenced, Johnny Keefler had been taken into the alley that had become so much a part of him. Anglio, Kowalcik and Caney took him into the alley, around the corner where no window could see. They did not kill him. Had they known it, their lives would have been easier to bear had they done so. They tied him to the iron stanchion of a fire-escape, gagged him and stripped him and worked on him for over three hours. After he was found hanging there unconscious, the interns who worked on him were sickened by what had been done to him, and marveled that he had been tough enough to survive it. They unwound the wires, and probed for the fragments of glass and the small rusty nails, and sewed ripped tissues and soothed the carefully burned initials and extracted the stumps of the broken teeth.

When he was able to answer questions, he said that he did not know who had worked him over. He had not recognized them. He could not identify them. He was ten years old, but there was nothing left of the child in his eyes. And never after that was there anything left of childhood. He was released from the Home when he was sixteen. He passed the examinations on the third try and got on the police list when he was twenty. He got his appointment when he was twenty-one, served his year of probation and acquired patrolman status.

After two years of traffic, he obtained a transfer to the Robbery Detail, and a promotion to patrolman first class, the highest rating he achieved in his police career. He was not the kind of cop who achieves promotion. He did not take orders well. He was frequently censured for excessive brutality when making arrests. But he did not take a dime of grift. In the view of his co-workers, he was embarrassingly, excessively honest. He lived in a cheap room in the Sink. He never married, never had time for the casual formalities of friendship. During off-duty hours he prowled the Sink, the implacable hunter, armed and alert. He was a superb marksman. During the times when he was in disfavor he would be given a walking beat in the farthest residential areas of Hancock. But when he was off duty, he was back in the Sink.

A very special transformation took place in that alley on that dreary day thirty-two years before. It was not iron that entered his soul. It was a corrosive acid, and the walls of the soul were impervious to it. In the beginning there were six names on the list. Annlie, Rollins, Rillyer, Gennetti, Kowalsik, Casey. Rillyer was knifed to death in a prison riot. While he was still in the Home, Rollins put a stolen car into a bridge abutment at ninety miles an hour.

His first killing was Red Annlie. According to the official report, Annlie was creating a disturbance in a bar where off-duty Patrolman Keefler had stopped in. Keefler had identified himself and arrested Annlie. As he was taking Annlie to the nearest precinct house, Annlie broke away and attempted to flee. Patrolman Keefler called on him to stop, fired one warning shot in the air and then fired at Annlie's legs. The shot carried too high and hit Annlie at the base of the spine. Annlie, a door-to-door salesman with a record of three arrests for minor offenses, died thirty-six hours later in Lakeview Charity Hospital.

There were three left.

Pete Casey, wanted for auto theft and extortion, was located by Patrolman Keefler in a third-floor apartment in a relatively good section of Hancock. He was armed. He inflicted a flesh wound on Patrolman Keefler, the bullet nicking the inside of Keefler's left thigh. Casey died on the way to the hospital with three slugs in his lower abdomen.

Theodore Gennetti, on his way home from work, walking home after a late shift at the Hancock Wire and Brad

34

Company, was arrested by Patrolman Keefler. Keefler reported that Gennetti was "acting suspiciously" and he decided to bring him in for questioning. Gennetti had served six years in State Prison at Alton. When Gennetti pulled a knife, Patrolman Keefler beat him into submission. Gennetti was operated on for a depressed fracture of the occipital bone, and died the following day of a massive cerebral hemorrhage. Patrolman Keefler was reprimanded and given a sixty-day suspension.

Only Gilbert Kowalsik left, and Keefler had learned he had gone to the West Coast. Kowalsik returned after Keefler had been a cop for fourteen years. He came back on vacation. He was a union official on the Los Angeles docks. Four days after his return his body was found in the lake and identified. The autopsy indicated Kowalsik had been tortured to death.

They were all gone, but the memory of the alley was vivid in Keefler's mind. It had not changed. The six were gone, but it seemed there were always others to take their places.

Keefler, healthy, and with no dependents and with no friends in the department, was picked up by one of the World War II drafts that took men in their thirties. Because of his police background he was made an M.P. As a sergeant in London in 1944 he was broken for a brutal beating administered to three enlisted men of the Eighth Air Force on leave, and was reassigned to a stockade where men convicted of minor offenses were held for punishment and retraining. Keefler and three other members of the station complement were implicated in the death of two enlisted men serving time for theft, and all four of them were cleared.

In 1947 Patrolman John Keefler was given an indefinite suspension for the beating of a man apprehended in a car reported stolen. Keefler and his partner, Corporal Richard Benedict, had spotted the license and forced the car to the curb. Through an error on the part of the dispatcher, the car had not been taken off the hot list when it had been recovered and returned to the rightful owner. The rightful owner, a Mr. Paul Keller, an engineer at a local radio station, had attempted to explain to Keefler when he was

pulled out of his car. Keefler misinterpreted Keller's agita-
tion as resistance and, while subduing him, had broken
three ribs and his jaw.

Keefler was reinstated after a five-month suspension.
Nine years later the amputation of his left hand as the
result of a gunshot wound rendered him unfit for further
duty. He was retired from the Hancock Police Force on a
pension and appointed a parole officer.

He stood on the corner four blocks from the Bronson
house and waited for a city bus. The stump ached where
it fitted into the socket of the artificial hand, and the skin
under the strap itched. He saw the white-faced kid standing, trembling, eyes wide, hands raised, the big .45 on the
floor at his feet. Again he felt the numbness in his left arm,
from fingertips to elbow, and again he brought the sight
pattern into slow clear focus, felt the jump of the .38 in
his right hand, saw the perfect blackness of the round hole
in the kid's white forehead in the same instant the impact
knocked the kid back against the wall to rebound and fall
boneless across the big automatic.

He could feel the weight of the Detective Special in the
side pocket of his jacket. He thought of Lee Bronson and
wanted to see him on his knees with his face split and the
big words forgotten, begging in the remembered language
of the Sink. Begging like they all begged. Like Kowalsik
had begged.

He saw the bus in the distance, coming through the
heat-waver over the asphalt of Sherman Boulevard. He
could feel the city around him, sweating and sighing and
settling toward the dusk and the night. This was better
than being a cop. This could be much better. They let them
out too fast, too soon. But they would come out and they
would find that it was just a slightly larger cage. They
would meet Johnny Keefler and then they would know
about the bars around the bigger cage.

The bus, on its way downtown, was nearly empty. He
stepped up, showed his pass, and went back to one of the
red plastic seats. Danny Bronson would find out just how
strong were the bars of his new cage. Until he showed up
it would be nice to call on the kid brother once in a

while. Keep him in line. It was a little disappointing the way Bronson had knuckled under so easily. Scared of his job. A big bastard, but soft all the way through. Even after Danny was picked up and sent back to Alton, it might be okay to stop around. Do a little checking. If the professor wanted to get his back up and knew how to go about it, he might make trouble. But it was a reasonable chance to take. It would be nice to stop around and talk to that Lucille, too.

He half shut his eyes and remembered just how her legs had looked. They were very vivid in his memory, the rounded tender way her tanned thighs had been pressed together, the cherub face on her knee, the little bones of the slender ankles.

He wondered how bad the professor wanted to keep his job. And how bad she wanted him to keep his job. No Bronson should have exclusive rights to a piece like Lucille. The way she looked, maybe he thought he had, but the odds said he didn't. He was too solemn and dignified for a Lucille. Big sad-faced bastard. Full of the long words. Just another punk from the Sink who ought to get a good shove right back into the Sink. Apparently that Brookton Junior College wasn't too careful about who they hired.

At least the vividness of the image of the lovely legs solved one problem of scheduling. He decided that after he checked in the office he would go drop in on Talliaferro at the hotel where he worked and lean on him a little and watch him sweat. Sooner or later Talliaferro would slip. Maybe the way Judson had slipped. God, how Rich had stood up for Judson! You would have thought Judson was his son or something. He remembered the scene in Rich's office, with Rich wringing his narrow hands and steaming his own glasses.

"But, Keefler! You must use discretion! You *have* to exercise judgment. Terry Judson has stayed out of trouble for over eighteen months. He'll be off parole in another four months. He's got a wife."

And Keefler had stared at him, registering shock. "Rich, you asking me to goof off on my new job? I can show it to you right in the book. It says if a guy goes into a public place and drinks in public, it's a violation of parole. I saw him myself. I got here a statement from the bartender that served him and a statement from one of the guys on the team."

"But Terry is on that bowling team. So he had a beer."

"It's a public place with a liquor license and he could have had a coke, couldn't he?"

"I'm going to have to ask you to drop it, Keefler. Your job isn't to hound these men."

And then it had been time for him to show his hand. "Richardson, I didn't come here for you to try to tell me how I should do or what I should do. I come here to tell you I turned Judson in. I got him picked up. I appear against him in the morning. I'm covering my list. You cover yours."

"I'll appear, too."

"Suit yourself," he said and walked out. The law was the law. He had the proof. He presented it. Terry Judson went back to finish out his term. Richardson nearly found himself in contempt of court.

So tonight, after squeezing some sweat out of Talliaferro, he decided he would drop in on Connie Judson again. She was a hefty healthy redhead, and the rearrest of Judson had taken all the steam out of her. It wasn't his fault she got the idea he could get Terry sprung again. She was willing to put out. There wasn't much life in her, but how much choice did a one-handed guy have? Her heavy freckled legs didn't compare with the professor's piece, but it was a very nice thing to lie there and have a cigarette and think about Terry Judson back in the box, and think how you put him there. When she cried she didn't make much noise.

How much choice would you have if you didn't lean on them a little? And Judson was just another punk. He had a habit of writing worthless checks when he got tight. And after he got out he'd get the habit again.

His hand ached—the hand that was gone. Sometimes he felt like they'd buried it under a heavy stone, a cold stone. He often wondered what they'd done with it.

God damn that kid!

All the bad ones deserved was a sudden death and a dirty one. As dirty as Kowalsik's.

He bit the inside of his cheek. "I'll get them all, Mose," he said to himself. "I'll get them all for you."

He could still feel the rough affection of the hand that had rumpled his no-color hair, had patted the shy head of a scared kid in the waiting room of the Home.

And he felt something weep inside when he saw again Mose's ashy face and helpless clutching hands.

"Every one of them, Mose."

Mose wore the face of Christ.

And they had done that thing to him.

They had all done it. The Bronsons and Judson and Talliaferro. The G.I.s in that stockade had done it too, and answered for it in yelps of anguish as the billy stick splintered shin bone.

Keefler warred against all the foulness in the world, against everyone who had helped hold the knife that had spilled Mose onto the dirty sidewalk of the Sink. In his mind, even Lee Bronson had helped hold that knife.

When he got off the bus his lips were moving and there was a quiet madness in his eyes. And he hit the artificial hand against his thigh so as to feel more clearly the aching and the pain.

CHAPTER THREE

Lucille Bronson

She paused in the living room, head tilted to one side, and tried to hear what that man named Keefler was saying to Lee, but the man kept his voice too low. In the silence of the small house she could hear the excited beat of her heart, the heavy high-placed thudding. There was no way of knowing how much or how little Keefler knew. She had not liked the look of him. He had mean, wise little blue eyes, and he had looked at her in a way that was too knowing.

She went back through the living room and into the bedroom, shrugged out of the beach coat and flung it on the chair. Her suit was nearly dry. She stepped out of her clogs, peeled her suit down and stepped out of it, walked through into the bathroom and hung it over the edge of the tub. She paused briefly in front of the mirror over the sink and looked at the puckered marks the tight bra built into the suit had made on her breasts.

When she walked back into the bedroom, she went to her bureau to get clean underthings, and then changed her mind as she realized that some slight tactical advantage might be obtained by remaining naked. That is, if Keefler knew anything and had told Lee. But she didn't know how Keefler could know anything.

It had only happened twice. But if Lee found out, it wasn't going to make him feel any better to know it had only happened twice, and the first time it was really sort of like an accident. One of those things that can happen and it's really nobody's fault. The only thing to show was from the first time, and that had been her lip swollen and the cut inside it where this tooth back here is turned a little crooked, the one the dentist said didn't matter be-

40

cause it didn't show and it would be hard to try to straighten it. The front ones had always been straight so there never had to be any of those braces.

She sat on the bench in front of her dressing table and put her heel up on the bench, soaked cotton in nail polish remover and began to take the old cracked nail polish from her toes.

There was no way that Mr. Keefler could possibly know she had seen Danny twice. Once about two weeks ago—no, it was a little more than two weeks because it was on Friday, on Friday in the morning and that would make it two weeks ago yesterday. He hurt her mouth and when Lee saw it she told him the thing she made up about it, about how she was getting the hat box down off the top shelf of the closet and it slipped and hit her in the mouth.

It was one of those things that just happened. It hadn't been meant to happen either time, either fifteen days ago or Thursday, the day before yesterday. But maybe he meant for it to happen Thursday because he didn't leave his car in front like before.

She remembered how it was when Danny stopped on that Friday morning. She remembered she'd set the ironing board up and she was ironing the candy-striped skirt, the one with the tricky little pleats that you had to be careful about. And the television was on in the living room. You could sort of follow what was going on by listening, even if it was kind of hard sometimes, and then if it sounded exciting, you could hurry in and look at it and then come back out when it got dull again. She remembered she had been ironing the candy-striped skirt on account of Ruthie was going to come by about two and they were going to go down to the matinee of that new Bill Holden one. She wanted to wear it on account of it was a stinking hot day and it was a cool skirt and, because Lee had the car, they were going to walk to the bus and once you got downtown it was another four blocks nearly to the State. So she had decided to wear the candy-stripe with just a half slip. The white rayon blouse was thick enough and full enough so she was going to get away without wearing a bra no matter if Ruthie did make

41

some smart crack about her bobbling all over the place. Ruthie made those cracks on account of if she didn't wear a bra she'd be all hanging down to her belt practically. It was funny Earl didn't pick up a good buy in a used car for Ruthie, seeing as how he worked at that business and could get a good one, but it looked like he was as stingy as Lee almost.

Anyway, it had been something after eleven, maybe a quarter after, and the skirt was nearly done when she heard the familiar creak of the middle step of the three steps up to the small back porch and then a big man just outside the screen door with the sun behind him so she couldn't tell who it was, even when the man said, "Hi, Lucille."

When she started to the door he pushed it open and came in and she saw it was Danny, Lee's brother. She didn't know him well, having seen him only two or three times and then Lee had been there and a lot of the time the two of them had talked about people she had never heard of. It felt kind of funny to be alone with him, because she couldn't keep from thinking about how he'd been in jail three times and he was really a kind of a gangster. She remembered how Lee had told her parents about his brother Danny and how they'd been so upset about it they'd practically wanted to call the whole thing off. Lee could have kept it to himself and saved all that trouble, but that was Lee for you. He always had to go ahead and do just what he thought was the right thing to do, no matter what it cost people.

She remembered the first time she had met Danny and how he was so different from what she had thought. She had thought maybe he would be sort of like George Raft or maybe the other type like Ernest Borgnine, but actually you couldn't have told about him, hardly. In one tiny little way he was a little like Van Johnson, but older and heavier and just a little bit beat-up looking.

So when he came in, she told him Lee wasn't home and he wouldn't even be home to lunch on account of he didn't have enough time on Fridays on account of his schedule to come home. But Danny kind of ignored that and sat on one of the kitchen chairs and told her to go right ahead with her ironing.

He was quiet and kind of funny-acting, and it made her feel funny to just keep right on ironing. She had felt conspicuous in that tight old pair of blue-jean shorts and the skimpy yellow halter and barefoot and all. She tried to make conversation with him, and went in and turned off the television and saw his car out there at the curb and came back and tried to talk some more, but he just sort of grunted and kept frowning and didn't seem to pay much attention. He was wearing a wonderful looking pair of slacks, pale gray with sharp creases and black stitching down the sides and on the pockets, and a blue cotton shirt with a white horizontal stripe, and short sleeves. His arms were big and brown, and his hands made his cigarette look small and very white.

She finished the skirt and put it on the hanger and she half expected him to jump up and try to help when she folded up the ironing board, but he just sat there, not watching her at all, but watching the pattern in the linoleum.

"Would you like a beer?" she had asked. "Or some coffee maybe?" You certainly couldn't tell he'd been in jail any three times, but you could tell he was worried about something.

He seemed to make up his mind, and he didn't even answer about the beer or the coffee. He snapped his cigarette all the way across into the kitchen sink and he looked right at her and he said, "I got a problem, Lucille, and maybe you're the answer, but I don't know. Anyway, you're the only one I've been able to think of."

"Well, I . . ."

"Don't try to give me any answers until I tell you about it. But first I've got to ask some questions. Can you keep something from Lee?"

She couldn't understand what he was driving at. "I . . . I guess so."

He looked at her keenly. "Is there anything you do keep from him? Is there anything you've kept from him?"

She felt her face get sort of hot and she said, "Yes."

He stood up. "I've cut myself a piece of something, and

43

I've got to have some protection." He took an envelope out of his hip pocket. It was a long envelope, sealed and folded double. He slapped it against the knuckles of his other hand. "I want this in a safe place. I can't give it to Lee. I know him too damn well. He'd open it and tell himself it was for my own good and he might do something stupid. You think you can hide this where he won't find it, and keep your mouth shut about it?"

"Y-Yes, Danny."

"It's insurance against anything happening to me. But suppose I'm dealing with somebody that gets too mad to be smart. Then something happens to me. As soon as you find out, then you take this to the cops. It will make good reading. You can open it and read it yourself before you take it. But don't you open it unless I'm dead."

"All right."

"I mean that. I don't think I'll get hurt so long as I got this kind of insurance, though. If everything goes just like I want it to go, I'll be back one of these days to pick it up. Will you do this for me?"

"Yes. I'll do it, Danny," she said and held out her hand, but he didn't give it to her.

"I want to know where you're going to put it, Lucille. Show me the place first."

She remembered the hiding place she used, the old brown shoulder bag that hung on one of the back hooks of the closet. Danny followed her into the bedroom and she showed him the purse. He shook his head. "I don't like it. Suppose you're out and you get a guy working in here. Maybe he takes it, or looks in it."

"Under the mattress? Lee wouldn't find it there."

He looked at her almost with contempt. "I'll look around, honey. I'll find a place." She followed him as he went through the house. They ended up back in the kitchen. On the counter top under the cabinets was a row of graduated metal containers, yellow with a design on each of three ducks on a pond, and each one labeled. He took the top off the largest one, the one that said flour.

"I don't imagine you do much baking."

"Not very much."

"This ought to do," he said. It was more than half full.

He took it over to the sink. She stood a half step behind him and watched him work the envelope down until it must have been near the bottom of the can. He dusted his hands over the sink. "Okay," he said. "Put it back."

She carried it over and put it with the others. He gave her a cigarette and lit it. He looked down into her eyes and it made her feel uncomfortable. "Don't open the envelope."

"I won't. You told me already."

"And I'm telling you again. You're my brother's wife, but this is important to me. It's more important to me than you are, honey. If I should come back for it, and it might be any day from now on, and it's been opened, I'm going to work you over a little. You understand?"

"First you ask me to do you a favor and then you start talking about beating me up."

"I just want to make sure you understand. I'm . . . glad you'll do it. You're the only one I could think of. I've sort of . . . cut loose from old ties."

She looked up at him and thought about how he had been in jail, and looked at how wide his shoulders were, and how he had a kind of nice, reckless, wild look, not like Lee. It was funny two brothers could be so different. It wasn't that anything should happen, but it just did. She knew that it started right there while they were looking at each other. The house was so quiet. And they didn't say anything. And she knew she should look away, but she just kept looking at him and he kept looking back. She felt her breath get shallower and her breathing get quick. She saw his chest lift as he breathed. In the socket of his throat, above the blue and white shirt, there was a curl of harsh blond hair. There was no sound but the buzz of the refrigerator and some distant traffic and the noises of small kids playing in one of the back yards.

When he took hold of her she expected it, but not the quickness and the roughness of his grasp. She started to squirm and fight him, scared then, and thinking of Lee and of marriage and all that. She writhed away from him and half fell back and her shoulders crashed against the cabinets and she heard a dish fall inside. That was when he hit her with the back of his hand across the mouth and she made a kind of moaning sound and fell into his arms. He half carried and half dragged her into the bedroom and she could not stop making that moaning sound, and her body felt all loosened as if all the tight muscles had come untied. He was rough and harsh and contemptuous with her, rougher than Lee had ever been. It was like being punished. But, when she could have sworn that she could not respond to treatment like this, her response came in a quick upward blinding spiral.

She lay there too exhausted to move and, with her eyes half shut, watched him fix his clothing, latch his belt tight, turn and stand over her and light another cigarette. He cursed her and he cursed himself. He labeled their foulness with words she had never heard before. He cautioned her about the envelope and he left. She heard his heavy step in the kitchen, the bang of the screen door, and a few seconds later, the slam of his car door and and the angry roar of the engine, the sudden yelp of tires as he started up.

A long time later she got up and put on her robe and phoned Ruthie and said she had a headache. She took a hot bath, and then put on different shorts and another halter and fixed the rumpled bed and got the board out again and did some more ironing. Every once in a while tears would start to run down her face. She didn't feel as though she was crying. It wasn't like crying. All of a sudden the tears would run again. It was like, long ago, when the dog, Taffy, was killed by a car. She wouldn't even be thinking of Taffy. She would be doing her home-work or she'd be talking to a friend on the phone and the tears would come out of no place and it was the tears that would make her remember Taffy.

After that she thought about Danny so much that it seemed to her that she thought about him every minute of the day. When she remembered what he had called himself and what he had called her, it gave her a hollow-tummy feeling of excitement.

But when he came back, the day before yesterday, came back while she was sitting on the front porch in the early afternoon reading a magazine, he nearly startled her out of her wits. He had come in the back and he came through the house without the slightest sound to the open front door and spoke her name. Her heart fluttered and felt as if it were trying to jump out of her chest.

She went in, and felt too shy to look directly at him. He said, "I should have known it when I got my first good look at you."

"What do you mean?"

"You know what I mean. Of all the guys in the world, he's the one who has to hook up with you, Lucille."

She looked at him then. He was grinning at her, but it wasn't a warm grin. "You made me do it."

"That's right, Lucille. I made you do it."

"Why don't you get your envelope and get out?"

"I don't want it yet. I want you to keep this, too." He handed her an unsealed envelope. "Go ahead. Look in it."

She looked at the packet of fifty-dollar bills, then stared at him, her eyes wide. "What's this for?"

"They've changed the name of the game on me. I got parole trouble. I've got to move a little different on my deal than I planned. There's a thousand there. Sort of a down payment like. It's traveling money, and the best place for it is here, I think. Here's what will happen. If things go perfect for me, I'll be back to pick up that other envelope and you can keep this one. If things go sour, I'll be back to get both envelopes and I'll be in a hurry. Put that one in that purse in the closet you showed me. If things go really sour, I'll be dead. Then you keep the grand and give the other envelope to the cops."

She told him she understood. She went into the bedroom. He followed and watched her hide the second envelope. She turned around and looked at him. She saw the contempt on his face. She jumped forward and locked her arms around his neck. He flung her about trying to shake her off, but she held tightly to him. And knew the instant when he changed his mind. It was just like the other time, only this time he didn't say anything. He didn't stand over the bed when he lit his cigarette. He turned when he was in the bedroom doorway and lit it there and looked at her nakedness the way a man would glance at dirt in the street, and then he was gone and this time the screen door closed quietly and she heard no car motor. After she had her tub and fixed her bed and put on fresh clothes, she took the money and arranged it on the bed, arranged the twenty bills in all kinds of different patterns, hummed softly to herself and played with the money until it was nearly time for Lee to be home. This time there weren't any tears, and she had the warm and satisfied little feeling that she had gotten even with Danny in some way, but she couldn't understand just how that could be.

Now, with all the polish removed, she began to paint the toenails of her right foot, starting with the little one. She sat in a limber way, without strain, the inside of her sharply crooked knee warm against the side of her face. Her dressing table had a center mirror as well as two side mirrors at an angle. She heard him and glanced into the side mirror on the right and saw him in the doorway, leaning against the frame, hand in the pocket of the faded khakis, his expression cold and thoughtful.

She looked back down at her foot and started on the nail of the third toe, working carefully. "It looks like your brother is in some kind of trouble," she said.

"He's got trouble. Maybe we've got trouble, too."

"How could we have trouble?"

She heard him cross the room behind her, heard the sound of the bed as he sat on it. When he spoke the harshness of his voice startled her. "Stop that damn nonsense and turn around. I want to talk to you."

"Just a minute till I finish."

"Now, damn it!"

She put the brush back in the bottle, sighed audibly, swiveled around so that she faced him. "I don't know what you got to get so hot about," she said, keeping her face still but searching his face for proof that Keefler could have told him anything.

"Why don't you put some clothes on?"

"Do I look disgusting or something?"

"Stop fencing with me, Lucille. Put some clothes on."

She gave him a mocking look. A sexy mocking look, like Grace Kelly had used in that picture where Cary Grant was a jewel thief, and he was being blamed for the way jewels were being stolen because they were using his

48

methods, but he'd given up stealing long ago and he had to prove it wasn't him. She and Ruthie had practiced that look, and she had got it down just right, Ruthie said. You put your eyelids part way down and looked slantwise and smiled in a way that sort of turned one corner of your mouth down. She leaned over, a long lithe stretching, and caught the sleeve of the beach coat and pulled it to her and slipped into it, and turned the collar up the way it looked the best and said, "Better, darling?" drawling the words out slow.

"You lied to Keefler," he said.

She felt uncertain then. He didn't look like Lee at all. He didn't look friendly. He was more like Danny all of a sudden. Her voice was pitched higher. "If that man told you something about me, he was lying!"

Instead of looking angrier, Lee suddenly looked very tired. "Seel, I don't expect you to understand this. But I'm going to take a stab at it. We've got security. Whether you believe it or not, I've got a certain position, and I'm given a certain amount of respect."

She caught at the opening for counterattack, an opening too wide to ignore. "Yes, you've got everything. You've got a big deal. In ten years maybe you'll be making as much as a good carpenter. I can't even buy a lipstick without your showing me all the figures about how much it costs to . . . "

"Shut up, for God's sake. And listen. Keefler isn't normal. There's something twisted about him. He treated me as if . . . as if I was some petty thief in a lineup."

"Didn't you explain how you're a big important man around Brookton Junior College, dear?"

"That doesn't work with Keefler," he said, ignoring her obvious sarcasm. "I never thought it was a mistake coming back here until now. I didn't plan on a Keefler. If he wants to make trouble for me, he can. He can use Danny as a lever. And he can use . . . something else that happened a long time ago. He can make it look bad. As long as we stay clean, he won't bother, I don't think. But it's damn important that we stay clean. He'll pick up Danny, or somebody will, and then Keefler will be off our neck. It's a bad break for Danny, and I'm damn sorry about it,

49

but it's his own fault. I sat there, Seel, and I saw you lie to him. I know when you lie. I've proved that to you before. You're a poor liar. A lot of time I don't bother. It isn't worth the squabble we have about it. But this time it's important. Get that through your head. This time it counts. When did you see Danny last?"

"Just like I told Mr. Keefler. The day after your birthday."

"Come off it, Lucille. You've seen him since then. And I have to know about it. Right now."

She looked at him and she saw the clear purpose in his eyes. She realized, with consternation, that she would have to tell him something. It was unthinkable that she should try to tell him the whole thing. It had to be just enough to satisfy him. And there would have to be enough detail to make it sound right. She felt, for the first time, a really sharp stab of guilt for what she had done with Danny. It was really a terrible thing. It was his own brother. You couldn't twist it all around like in a movie and make it seem better. It was something she hadn't done before, and hadn't planned to do. Ruthie talked about it a lot, but with Ruthie it was all talk. In a way it was Lee's fault it happened. He seemed to think he could stick her in this crummy little house on Arcadia Street and keep her on a silly budget and have her be happy forever. When you were used to a lot of things going on, a lot of laughs and so on, you couldn't be expected to adjust to a life where a faculty tea was a big deal.

"Come on," Lee said insistently. "Out with it."

Her mind moved quickly, sorting, editing, discarding. "Well, I did see him. But I made a promise."

Lee sighed. "The whole story. Come on."

"Well, it was two weeks ago yesterday. I only saw him that one time. It was in the morning and I was ironing and he came to the back door. He seemed worried about something. I told him you weren't here and he said he wanted to ask a favor of me. He said he was in some kind of trouble. He wanted me to keep something for him, to hide it here in the house. He said he didn't want to ask you to do it because you'd have a lot of questions and so on. So I promised him I would."

"Did he come back for it, whatever it was?"

"No. He was just here that one time. I've still got it."

"Go get it."

She stood up, thinking of going to the kitchen, to the canister of flour, and she remembered how insistent Danny had been about not opening it, and his promise about what he would do if she did. So she turned instead toward the closet, pushed the clothes aside, took the envelope of money from the brown purse and, in a sudden rage at her own stupidity in not taking any of the money out, she flung the envelope at Lee. The money spilled in the air and fluttered down around him, on the bed and on the floor, and she wanted to laugh at his dazed expression.

He picked the money up slowly, counted it and put it back in the envelope. "A thousand dollars," he said.

"What for?"

She sat on the bench again. "He said he was in trouble and it was getaway money if things didn't work out right. But if they did, we could keep it. And if he got killed, we could keep it."

"He didn't say what kind of trouble?"

"You know how he is."

"And that was all?"

"He gave it to me to hide and told me not to tell you about it and then he left."

"Did he park his car in front?"

"No. I don't know where he left it. He came to the back door. I was in the kitchen ironing. He went out the back door when he left."

"Have you told anybody about this? Did you tell your friend Ruthie?"

"No. I haven't told anybody."

Lee sat, frowning, and he rapped the envelope against the knuckles of his other hand. It was the same gesture Danny had used.

"What are you going to do?" she asked.

"I don't know. I'm trying to guess how Keefler would react if I told him what . . ."

"But it's your own brother!"

"I'm aware of that, Seel. I'm very aware of that, believe

51

me. But I have to be sure Keefler won't get on the trail of this . . . incident. I guess we have to take a chance."

"Shall I put it back?"

"I'll take care of it, thank you. Seel, why couldn't you have told me about this when it happened."

"I promised Danny. I gave my word."

"You're married to me. I don't like Danny roping you in on something like this."

"Where are you going to put it? Suppose he comes after it when you aren't home?"

"You tell him to wait and you phone me at the school and I'll come back as soon as I can."

"Suppose he's in a hurry?"

"That is going to be too damn bad. I want to know what the hell is going on." He walked toward the bedroom door, turned and said, "I've got a meeting at seven."

"I don't know how you expect to use up all the time there is asking me all kinds of questions and then think I can push a magic button and have a meal pop out of the wall or something in two seconds. I was real stupid. I was thinking it was Saturday night and maybe it wouldn't be too much to expect to get taken out, maybe, and even . . ."

"Skip it, skip it," he said. "I'll get a sandwich on the way."

When he came back into the bedroom she was working on the other foot. He showered quickly and changed. By the time he was ready to leave she had nearly finished shaving her legs.

"I'll be back about eight-thirty," he said.

"Oh, goody," she said, not looking up.

"Maybe we could go out to the drive-in."

"Double goody."

"Think it over," he said. He put his hand on her shoulder and she turned a sullen face up for his kiss, turning her lips aside so that his mouth brushed her cheek. He started to say something else, then turned and left the room. She heard the thin slap of the screen door, the whine of the feeble starter, the fading sound of the noisy motor. The room was turning gray-blue with dusk. She went out and phoned Ruthie, but there was no

answer. She went sulkily into the kitchen, made herself a
peanut butter sandwich and ate it standing at the sink.
The kids next door were having a screaming contest. After
she drank a glass of milk she began to look for the
money. It took her half an hour to decide it was in his
desk drawer, the middle drawer, and it was locked. She
worked at the lock with a bent paperclip for a long time,
and gave up in disgust.

She turned on the television, checked the six available
channels, turned it off. She looked in her purse and found
she had two dollars and a quarter. The evening was
beginning to get cool. She put on her powder blue suit
and walked down to the bus stop. She left the house un-
locked, left no note. Let him sweat. Let him go to the
drive-in by himself. She saw the bus coming, and she felt
as though she wanted to cry. The night was full of people
having fun. And there wasn't any fun left over for Lucille.

CHAPTER FOUR

Danny Bronson

Danny woke up at eleven on Sunday morning,
the fourteenth of October. He had had another
prison dream, full of stone and bars and naked
lights and night noises. He brought it out of sleep with
him, and it took him long seconds to reorient himself in
time and place, to identify the slant of beamed céiling
above him. He raised up on one elbow and looked at the
clock and lighted the first cigarette of the day.

It was an enormous and comfortable bed with a trick
headboard with radio, bookshelves, light switches. He ex-
haled, lay back, and felt the dull pulsation of a mild
hangover. Too much liquor, too many cigarettes, and
maybe a little bit more than enough of the big brunette,
Mrs. Drusilla Catton, who had installed him in this remote
and luxurious private lodge and expected frequent and
earthy attentions in return.

Drusilla had explained to Danny why the camp was so
luxurious and so isolated. Drusilla was the thirty-year-old
second wife of Burt Catton, aged sixty. Burt had built the
camp long ago when the first Mrs. Catton had been alive.
Burt had originally picked up the sixteen hundred acres of
forest land with the idea of subdividing it. But, because
Ethel, the first Mrs. Catton, was almost impossible to
endure without some systematic diversion, he had built
the camp in great secrecy, a place for private and special
entertainment unsuspected by the dread Ethel. It was
sixty-three miles from Hancock—sixty on Route 90, then
three on a narrow county road. The final half mile was a
private gravel road. He had brought in electricity, had an
earth dam built to convert a stream into a two-acre lake,
and had gone as far afield as Toledo to import an

architect who seemed to have an instinctive understanding of just what Burt Catton wanted. Local labor from the near-by town of Kemp had constructed the camp. It was on a knoll overlooking the two-acre pond, with a good view of a range of far hills beyond the pond. The roof had the steep pitch and big overhang of structures where the snow load is heavy. The house was a rectangle, with but two huge rooms, the living room and the bedroom. A narrow hallway connected the two rooms, with a tiny kitchen off one side of it and an equally small bath off the other side.

Many windows in both the living room and the bedroom faced the pond. With its paneled walls, subdued dramatic lighting, deep furniture, startling color contrasts, efficient bar-corner, luxurious music system, low tables, chunky ash trays, the house served Burt Catton's purposes perfectly. There were obvious clues to what those purposes had been: the vastness of the bed, the curious profusion of mirrors in the bedroom, the lack of provision for guests, the absence of any personal belongings. Dru had told him how she had been brought here by Burt, after Ethel had died but before Burt had married her, how he was known locally as Mr. Johnson, how one big closet in the bedroom was filled with dressing gowns and night gowns of a spectacular sheerness.

It had served as a refuge for Burt Catton during the final years of Ethel's vituperative life—a place she did not know about, a place where she could not reach him. He had sometimes come here alone, but more often he was accompanied by a woman.

When Ethel Catton had died at sixty-one, leaving her husband, one married son and one married daughter, Burton Catton had been fifty-six. He was a heavy, brown, bearlike man, loud, virile, friendly, full of lusty appetites, a man of prominence and position in Hancock. Though it was known that Ethel Catton, who had been a Brice, had been well off when he married her, it was also commonly known that Burt, shrewd, hungry and sometimes ruthless, had done well in his own right. Some said he had more than trebled her money.

Two years after Ethel's death, Burt Catton, then fifty-eight, had quietly married Drusilla Downey, twenty-eight-year-old daughter of Calder Downey, an ineffectual man of good family who was slightly affronted at being presented with a son-in-law six years his senior. But he was glad to have Drusilla off his hands. It was her third marriage. The first had occurred when she was seventeen to an inept New Jersey prizefighter called, most incongruously, Panther Rose. It had ended in annulment. Her second marriage at twenty-two to a quiet young man of twenty-six, a promising lawyer in a large Hancock firm, had ended three years later when the young man had taken his own life.

Calder Downey hoped that Burt Catton could control Drusilla. He sensed the strength in Catton that might make this possible. Calder knew Drusilla was not an evil person. The nearest he could come to a diagnosis was to say that she did not seem to give a damn. She was dark, reckless, full-bodied, hot-blooded, a woman who drank too much, drove too fast, borrowed constantly against her trust fund income, slept with anyone who attracted her, was casual about her dress, yet managed to extract an uncompromising loyalty from her friends. At twenty-eight the marks of the hard and headlong pace were beginning to show.

Two years after their marriage, two years after the long honeymoon spent in the redecorated camp, Burt Catton had a serious coronary. Four months later he was able to get around again. He was forty pounds lighter, gray rather than brown, withered, trembly, too scared to bend over and pick up his hat if he dropped it. That was the only year of their lives when Dru would be precisely half his age. The attack had changed Burt Catton into an old man who thought a great deal about death and could find no strength within himself to adjust to its inevitability. For a man of his intelligence he had managed to live an astoundingly long time with an inner conviction of immortality. During his enforced rest, his always tangled affairs had gotten into a dangerous condition. He had always had more than enough energy to control many ventures simultaneously. During the weeks he lay in bed, several important and promising things went sour. He could not think of specific instructions to give his lawyers. And so nothing was done. Before his attack, a tax decision altered a previous capital gains profit to income, and it was necessary to liquidate certain property holdings to pay even part of the assessment.

He came slowly up from his closeness to death, and found himself with a wife who had been the beloved of the man he had once been. But this smaller, slow-moving, apprehensive man could feel no closeness to her. He felt no need to impose his will on her. He knew she was drinking too heavily, that she was bored and restless and looking for trouble. It seemed incredible to him that less than a year ago when she had annoyed him, he had yanked her, kicking and screaming and cursing him, down across his lap, had flipped up her skirt, ripped off the wisp of nylon panties and, with laughing gusto and sensual pleasure, applied the hard palm of his hand to the rounded ripeness of creamy buttocks until pain leached the fury out of her, until she wept with all the limp, deep satisfaction of the child who knows punishment was merited. She had eased herself gingerly down into chairs for the next few days, and she had been very meek and dutiful, and very affectionate. He wished he had known enough to apply the same wisdom and the same vigorous chastening measure to Ethel long long ago.

But after he was up and around again, moving with the brittle caution of the elderly and the frightened, it did not seem possible to him that he could have ever cowed Dru in such a way. She looked bigger and sturdier, and her voice seemed louder. He bowed to her fits of temper and tried not to hear her, and wished she would leave him alone. She was neither important nor necessary. It was important to think about the money, to think about it calmly and logically and effectively, or else be plucked clean.

He spent a lot of time with Paul Verney. Paul had taken some chilling losses too. And it became clear to them that they needed a coup, a coup of a specific nature. It had to result in a large dollar profit in a very short time, and the profit had to be in cash, and it would have to be a profit that need not be declared.

Any other venture was purposeless.

Paul found the method, made the contacts. Burt Catton was frightened by the risk. But he was more frightened by what his heart might do under the constant strain of worry. He had never touched anything so dangerously illegal. But he agreed. Paul went ahead. And, one night, very depressed, apprehensive, looking for both understanding and reassurance, he told Drusilla the whole story.

And two weeks later Drusilla told Danny. She told him just a little bit. Enough, she thought, to intrigue him. Just a delicate hint. She had no intention of telling him all of it. But she did tell him, stammering in her eagerness to get all the words out, pain bleaching her lips.

Danny butted his cigarette and got up out of the oversized bed. He walked to the window and looked at the thermometer fastened outside. Sixty-three. And the water would be colder. He went through to the living room and opened the door and walked, naked, out onto the small flagstone terrace. There were red October leaves on the flagstones and on the blue top of the metal table, and on the plastic webbing of the terrace chairs. He walked down the path to the pond, a broad powerful man with a hirsute body. He padded out the length of the dock and dived awkwardly and without hesitation into the chill water. He thrashed out into the middle of the pond, breathing hard, circled and swam back, clambered up onto the dock and walked back up to the camp, shivering. He rubbed himself dry with a big fluffy towel with an ornately embroidered C in the corner. He shaved, dressed in chocolate brown slacks and a white sports shirt and a yellow cashmere cardigan Dru had bought him.

He carefully prepared an ample breakfast and took it on a tray out into the sun on the terrace. He sat with his cigarettes and his pot of coffee and tried to make himself feel calm all the way through, tried to stop the fluttering that came and went. Verney would play. He had to play. He had no other choice. This was the big one. And it was going to go right, and he was going to go a long way away from here, away from a diligent little man named Keefler.

This was the sort of deal he had dreamed about. And

58

had never believed he would get close, this close. Before his release in May he had done a lot of thinking. It was painful thinking, because it showed him just how little he had done with his life. At thirty-two there wasn't much to look forward to. He knew that Kennedy would put him on. There were always things Kennedy could use him for. There was always a call for a muscle. It would be a couple of bills a week. But inevitably, inexorably, there would be a fourth fall at the end of it. And the tag of an habitual. And a long long term. He wouldn't be worth the best protective efforts of Kennedy's legal talent. He would be discarded, with slight regret.

He got out and went to work for Grunwalt and, very carefully and politely, he ignored the feelers that Kennedy's people put out. But as the weeks went by he had the sick feeling that sooner or later he would rejoin the organization. There didn't seem to be anything else he could do. He dreamed up and discarded dozens of ideas for a solo operation.

Then, in the last week in June, he attended a party in a big apartment given by a city official whose ties to both Bouchard and Kennedy had been close and profitable. There were many familiar faces there. Kennedy's people seemed to think it just a matter of time before he came back into the fold. It was at that party he met Drusilla Downey Catton. It was late in the evening. Her escort had passed out and been stowed in one of the bedrooms with the other casualties. By then Danny was tight enough to decide to take over where the previous one had left off. Drusilla was a big handsome vital woman of about thirty, dark-haired and colorful, with a strong face, an air of recklessness, an inexplicable air of importance, and a voice and way of speaking that made him think of Katherine Hepburn.

They took their drinks out onto a terrace that overlooked the city and the lake, and she hoisted herself up to sit on the wide cement wall sixteen stories above Lake Drive. She talked and he listened, at first with mild interest and then a growing excitement. She had barely known the man who had brought her. Her husband was Burton Catton. Danny knew him as a much older man, a man of money and importance. She said Catton had had a severe heart attack and was so concerned with taking his own pulse that he had no time for her. She said she was perfectly fascinated by the party and by all the types she had met. These people seemed so very much more interesting than her circle of dull friends. Actually they made her friends seem quite bloodless. Was it really true that that one named Al Altamiro had his left arm *shot* off? Danny told her how it had been amputated by a twelve-gauge shotgun during a union jurisdictional dispute, and she was delighted to know the details, and she quivered deliciously. He sensed that she was bored, reckless, restless —that she lived for excitement and sensation. And he knew there was money behind her.

Consequently, when she began to ask about him, he did not conceal the truth as he would have with a different sort of woman. He told the truth and embellished it. He gave himself a bloodier background than was reasonable. In actual fact he had committed but one murder, and that had been unintentional. He'd been ordered by Bouchard to discipline a runner who had been holding out on his numbers take. The dim light of the room where he had beaten the man had put his aim off, and a blow to the mouth had crushed the throat and the runner had strangled to death. After the embarrassing problem had been solved by slinging the body under a slow-moving freight, Bouchard had been annoyed with Danny until he became aware that the end result had been a remarkable increase in the efficiency of the other runners. And one time, because of his driving skill and his knowledge of the city, he had driven for two specialists who had been imported to take care of a gambler named Berman. Berman had learned he had an incurable cancer, and in addition to making his peace with his God, a move to which Nick could not object, Berman also wanted to cleanse himself with the Grand Jury, a procedure which could not be permitted. The more important of the two imported trigger men was a sulky, sleepy little man who, due to his fondness for and accuracy with a Colt .22 Woodsman fitted with a German silencer, was known as Peashooter. Danny, at the wheel, heard the husky sound, hardly louder than a snapping of the fingers, and learned an hour later, after he had garaged the car, that Berman, drinking coffee in his kitchen, had taken the slug directly in the orifice of the right ear—which, considering his condition, might be counted as a favor.

But, with Drusilla Downey Catton, he dwelt on his three prison terms, hinted at the direness of his deeds, and dredged up convincing detail from the welter of shop talk he had been hearing all his life. And he was not unaware that the more dangerous he made himself, the more delight Dru took in her delicious shudderings, and the more insistent became the pressure of her round warm leg against his hip as they talked there on the terrace. This was a phenomenon he had heard about, but had never experienced, the fascination of the wellborn woman with a pronounced sexual drive for the fighter, the thug, the jockey.

He took her for the first time that same night, on a woolly blanket spread beside her convertible, some fifteen miles from the city. He was as rough with her as he expected she desired him to be. And he learned she was a great deal of woman.

They spent the following evenings together, and at the end of the week he quit his job, gave up his room, and, on the first day of July, was installed out at the camp. The heart attack had made it most unlikely that Burt Catton would ever go near the camp again. In essence Danny knew that he was simply at stud. It was all that was expected of him, but in the case of Drusilla Downey Catton, that was a requirement almost heroic. On the first of July she had received the semiannual installment from her trust fund. After paying off her debts there was enough left for her to buy him an almost new car, more clothes than he had ever owned before, stock the camp with ample liquor and great boxes of food, provide him with pocket money. He had never lived better or been lonelier. This was not the deal he had planned for himself, but it was much more pleasant than working for Grunwalt.

In order for the relationship to be palatable to both of them, it was necessary that certain fictions be devised. He told her that, due to the long memories of certain enemies, it was healthier for him to be in such an isolated place. Also it gave him a chance to plan some big operation. She was providing the place for him because it wasn't being used anyway. She was a woman of frightful energies. She could slip out of the great bed at one in the morning and be back, fresh, eager, glowing with health, demanding his immediate attentions, at eight the next morning. Her eyes had the slight bulge, her throat the faint tell-tale fullness of the hyperthyroid. After a time Danny Bronson began to wonder how long he could last.

And then he found the big chance had been right in his lap. She had questioned him about the big job he was supposed to be planning. She never tired of listening to his shop talk. Then she said, "It isn't fair, really, you know. Because I mean they'll look for someone like you, won't they? But *respectable* men, like Burt and Paul Verney, they can get away with a dreadful thing without anybody knowing."

"What do you mean?"

"Oh, it's something they're doing. It depends on getting rid of some money. Quite a lot of money."

He had tried to question her, but she turned arch and mysterious. Lately she had been slowly achieving a position of dominance over him. She had begun to give orders and expect them to be obeyed. He had been the dominant one in the beginning. He had roughed her up from time to time. Not seriously. Never marking her. She seemed to enjoy it and expect it. But this was different.

It did not take him very long. Nerve centers and pressure points are much the same for a woman as for a man. With the flood of genuine agonizing pain came a fear that oiled her face and turned it gray. He had her in a corner and he made the words tumble out of her, a gasping torrent. Then, holding her arm, he walked her gently to the big bed. She walked with the feeble fragility of a very old woman. When the pain had faded, he made her tell him again, and asked her questions until he was certain he knew all she knew. The harsh discipline had shocked her. It made her very meek and highly affectionate. It restored him to the place of dominance.

His original plan had been to move slowly, and, using the startling information Dru had given him, milk Verney and Catton with restraint so as not to alarm them too much. He made his required phone calls to Richardson.

But then Keefler came into the picture. And suddenly, unexpectedly, he became a parole violator, a wanted man, a man owing the state over seven years. He would be forty upon release. If there was a single truth in all the world, it was this: They would never take him back.

And it changed his approach to Verney and Catton. He had to take big and take fast. He had to squeeze them, and protect himself in the process. The letter in the flour canister in Lucille's kitchen was insurance. The thousand he had dropped off on Thursday was another kind of insurance. When he thought of Lucille it made him feel soiled. Silly bitch. Lee deserved the best, not a round-heeled bag like that. She looked right at him and asked for it, just as obviously as any woman can ever ask for it. And he'd been too damn weak to ignore it. He prayed Lee would never find out. But sooner or later Lee would find out about her. It would happen with somebody else and he'd find out, and then if the timing was wrong, Lee would kill her.

Verney was due at two o'clock. Another hour to wait. Another hour to go over it carefully, so he would say the right things to Verney. The man had a lot of control. You had to give him that. Danny had taken the chance of driving into town on Thursday. He had phoned Paul Verney at his office at nine-fifteen and managed to brush off the insistent secretary and get through to Verney.

"My name is Bronson. You don't know me, Mr. Verney. But I want to see you just as soon as I can on a matter of importance."

Verney had a deep voice, careful articulation. "I'm afraid I have a very full schedule, Mr. Bronson. Perhaps you can give me some idea of what this is all about."

"I'll mention two names and then maybe you can guess what it's all about. Catton. Rovere." There was no answer. "Mr. Verney?"

"I am still on the line, Bronson." The deep voice was calm and precise. "I can see you at ten."

Verney's suite of offices was on the sixth floor of the Market Building at the corner of George and Castel Streets. On the opaque glass of the door was lettered *Paul D. Verney, Attorney at Law*. The offices were small, hushed, quietly and effectively furnished. The girl spoke almost in a whisper when she said, "Through that door, Mr. Bronson. He's expecting you."

When Dru had described him, she had said, "He's a big gaunt type, sort of funereal, I suppose. Great dignity and presence. Rusty clothes and hollow eyes. I'll bet he collects Lincolniana. He and Burt have been mixed up on all kinds of deals for years and years. He got clipped in this same tax decision that hurt Burt. A huge bite plus penalties and interest for five years."

Verney was sitting behind his desk when Danny walked in. Dru had been right, up to a point; but Verney was much younger than Danny had guessed—perhaps in his early forties. And he had expected pallor and fragility. Though Verney was lean, he had tremendous hands and wrists, sloping powerful shoulders and a look of fitness.

"Please sit down, Mr. Bronson. That was a very mysterious message. I must confess it intrigued me. Cigar?"

"Thanks." Danny bit off the end, spat it onto the rug, lit it with the silver lighter Dru had given him. He leaned back and smiled at Verney and told Verney precisely what he was doing, what Verney and Catton were planning. He watched Verney closely and saw no change of expression, no tightening of the mouth.

"And just where would you get this curious story?"

"From Catton's wife. He told her the whole thing."

Verney nodded. "I see. If this story was correct, what would be your next step?"

Danny told him exactly what he wanted. Again Verney nodded quite casually. "If this story happened to be correct, you understand that I couldn't give you an answer here and now."

"I realize that. Suppose you come out and see me."

"Where are you located?"

"Catton's camp. Out near Kemp."

For the first time he saw an unguarded flicker of surprise. It faded quickly. "Sunday? About two?"

"That will be fine, Mr. Verney. But I want to make one thing clear. I've got my guard up. Way up. The whole thing has been written down. It's in a safe place. It goes to the cops the minute I stop reporting in."

"That would seem to be a sensible provision, Mr. Bronson."

"I thought so."

"Until Sunday, then."

It disappointed Danny that he had made so little impression on the man. Verney's iron control was distressing to him. So, on the spur of the moment, he said, "You people use retainers. I'd like a little retainer. Call it a sort of guarantee of good faith."

"How much, Mr. Bronson?"

"A thousand."

Verney had nodded. They had walked together to the bank, a block away. He had waited while Verney cashed a check, came over to him and gave him the envelope containing twenty fifty-dollar bills.

Danny said, "At least you admit I got the right dope."

"We shall have our discussion on Sunday, Mr. Bronson."

"Come all by yourself. Know the way?"

"I have been there before. Good day, Mr. Bronson."

Verney arrived at the camp at ten after two, driving a black four-year-old Dodge. Danny heard the car and walked out and saw Verney park beside his car and get out. Verney wore a dark blue unpressed suit and a dark grey felt hat.

There was, of course, no handshake. They sat at the blue metal table on the terrace. Danny said there was hot coffee and Verney said he would appreciate some, thank you, no cream or sugar. Danny went in and brought out the cups, saucers and pot on a tray. Verney acted as though he were handling a matter for a client, something in which he was not involved personally.

Danny poured the coffee and sat down.

"Mr. Bronson, I have given your proposition a great deal of thought. I have not, as yet, mentioned or discussed the matter with Mr. Catton. I felt that it would be more to the point if we could discuss this matter calmly and arrive at some more equitable solution."

"I'm not going to dicker."

"I am assuming you are a reasonable man. I am assuming that you have a certain amount of intelligence, and that you can be objective about this situation."

"I'll listen to you."

"Both Mr. Catton's and my personal financial affairs are in extremely bad shape. We are in certain ventures together, and we both have interests in other unshared ventures. Our problem is largely one of timing. I have managed to explain this to the tax people in a manner that has satisfied them to the extent that they will delay taking liens on our property and holdings. We entered on this risky venture, the one you became advised of, as a means of acquiring a large amount of cash."

"Illegally."

"Yes, of course. But the risk, up until the moment you phoned me, seemed worth taking. We estimated that, after dividing the profit from this venture, we could more than satisfy our tax indebtedness, and thus hold onto other quite promising ventures until they in turn prove out. Now let us take a look at what will happen if we meet your demand. We will not be able to pay the tax indebtedness. All tangible and intangible holdings will be seized. Both Mr. Catton and myself will be penniless, and with future earnings highly obligated. And it is very difficult to frighten a penniless man, Mr. Bronson. Mr. Catton and I were able to scrape together sixty-five thousand dollars. Let us say we both had a cash reserve for contingencies. We could have paid it against the tax, but instead we decided to invest it in this venture you learned about. To accede to your demand would not only eliminate all chance of profit but would give us an additional net loss of sixty-five thousand. Frankly, one of the reasons I did not confer with Mr. Catton before coming here was because I am not at all sure it wouldn't kill him."

"I don't know what the hell you're driving at, Verney."

"This is an appeal to reason. If you persist in being stupidly greedy, you will get nothing."

"And you and Catton will go to jail. I've been there. You won't like it."

"Possibly. I don't think Burt would live to be sentenced. And I can think of several ways I might avoid a sentence. It's a chance I believe I'm willing to take."

Danny watched Paul Verney. It was impossible to tell whether the man was bluffing. "What's the counter offer?"

"Patience. Let us go ahead with the marketing the way we planned it. We will move slowly but safely. In that way we can hope to obtain full face value. That means a cash profit of two hundred and sixty-two thousand. You will be cut in for a full third, or a bit more than eighty-seven thousand. That is a good deal of money, Mr. Bronson. It may, in fact, be more than you will realize if you should take the entire amount and attempt a sale at a discount. You will remember that we purchased the entire amount for only sixty-five thousand. Frankly, I believe this is a generous offer, and I advise you to accept it."

"Wouldn't that be a little stupid of me? Once you market it, where am I? What can I prove?"

"During the interim, you will be in possession of a detailed confession signed both by Mr. Catton and myself. You will, of course, relinquish this when you receive your share. In addition, Mr. Bronson, may I point out that as far as you know, the money may be out of reach already. What would prevent me from burning it, for example? Wouldn't that be preferable to a jail sentence?"

"I'll tell you just why we're going to play my way, Verney. And why there's no other way I will play it. First, I'm wanted. I took a risk going into town. I'm not going in again. I'm wanted for violation of parole. I owe the state over seven years. Bronson is my right name. Danny Bronson. I'll tell you that because there's not a damn thing you can do with it. Second, I've got it all planned out. I've got a contact in Chicago. I can get a very nice passport and get it fast. And I know exactly where to go. I'll fly and I'll go to Turkey, and I'll take the money with me. I won't have to market it. I can use it there at face value. There's no such a thing as extradition from Turkey."

"I'm aware of that. Are you aware of the fact you've improved my bargaining position?"

Danny saw Verney smile for the first time. It was a broad smile. It was as cold as the underside of a frog. "What do you mean?"

"I won't accept ruin. I refuse to accept that. I swear this. I swear it before all I hold sacred, Daniel Bronson. Either make your demand reasonable, or I shall destroy every trace of that money. Then you can serve your seven years, and Catton can die, and I can slowly but certainly work my way out of indebtedness. You can not and will not frighten me. I decided that the moment I hung up the phone after your call."

Danny looked directly into the deepset eyes. "Burn it up, Verney. Get rid of it. You know exactly how hot that money is. It's been the hottest money in the country for better than three years. All I have to do is let the word out to the F.B.I. They'll bring in a flock of guys. They'll backtrack you to wherever you got it. They'll prove you got hold of it. Don't think they won't. And then it won't matter a damn whether you burned it or not. Want to keep playing this game?"

Verney leaned back. His voice was slightly weak as he said, "You're a very difficult man, Bronson."

"We've both played a lot of poker. But I can see the hole you're in, and I don't want you doing anything damn foolish, and I don't want Catton doing anything stupid. I can see that I've got to leave you some bait. I'll go this far. I want two hundred thousand. A hundred and ninety-five can be the hot stuff, but I want five I can use anywhere, in small stuff. That will leave you . . . let me see . . . a hundred and thirty-two thousand of the hot stuff. You can get rid of it through your channels and still double your investment."

"That isn't going to be enough."

"You're going to have to get along with it. Hell, if you're really in the bag, why not screw Catton, take all that's left and do like I'm going to do? You can live good, they tell me."

"It isn't enough."

"I'm giving you a break and you better take it."

68

Verney raised one heavy eyebrow. "Or else?"

"Or else. That's it. Or else you get smashed no matter what happens to me. I can do seven standing on my head. You bring it out here Wednesday. I can wait until then. Then bring it, and don't be short. Don't be a dime short. And you can't afford to get any fancy ideas because, as I told you before, it's all written down and in a safe place."

Verney looked down at his big-knuckled hands for a long time. At last he nodded.

"All right."

"Wednesday?"

"Wednesday afternoon."

"I won't stay around long after that."

"Is Mrs. Cotton going with you?"

"She thinks so."

He stood up. "She is a stupid, shallow woman."

Danny watched the Dodge drive away, down the gravel road and around the bend and out of sight behind the trees. He went into the house, put two ice cubes in a glass and covered them with bourbon. He walked into the bedroom, grinned into the largest mirror and silently toasted himself.

CHAPTER FIVE

Paul Verney

Though Verney knew that the trouble had started only a year ago, it seemed to him that things had been going wrong all of his life. Each cumulative disaster required a more desperate counter measure. In the past he had been able to depend on Burt Catton, on Burt's extroverted optimism, his nimble unscrupulous mind.

But now Burt was gone and in his place there was a grave, withered, apprehensive little man, subject to tears of weakness and moods of dark depression. How could Burt have been such a fool as to tell Drusilla? Everything had been handled so carefully.

He drove sedately back toward Hancock, and he remembered how proud he had been of the extreme care he had used. There was no one who could prove definitely that he had driven to Tulsa, and that he had returned with the money locked in the trunk of this same car. For three years and more the nation had wondered what had happened to the money in the Rovere case. He had followed the news reports at the time it had happened. He would have been both very frightened and most indignant if anyone had told him at that time he would ever have that money in his possession.

Calvin Rovere had been a wealthy resident of Houston, a man who had made many millions in oil, ranch land and trucking lines, a big hearty man who had married in his early forties, married a very pretty girl from Fort Worth. A little over a year after their marriage twin sons were born, and, two years later, a daughter. Rovere maintained a summer place in the hill country north of San Antonio, a large but otherwise unpretentious house on fifteen acres of land in a bend of the Guadalupe River near Bandera. He had a good airstrip put in, and during the hot months he commuted. On a Wednesday in August his wife flew down to Houston with him one morning and spent the day shopping, leaving the children at the summer place, along with a cook, a maid, a foreman and three hands. The twin boys were nine, the daughter seven.

Some time during the afternoon the twin boys disappeared. One man reported that he had seen a battered station wagon stop on one of the side roads bordering the place at about two o'clock. He could not tell the make. It was too far away to see how many people were in it. He forgot the incident and did not remember it until midnight when, under the stress of direct questioning by a captain of the Rangers, he recalled the incident. In the morning a piece of brown wrapping paper weighed down by a stone was found inside the fence line where the station wagon had stopped. On it was printed in pencil, *If you want to see your kids alive get together a half million dollars in small unmarked bills and wait till you hear from us.*

Rovere, with considerable difficulty, managed to collect the sum required without attracting the attention of the press. Police work on the case was discreet and good. After the necessary seven days were up, the F.B.I. was called in. No word had been received from the kidnapers. After staff conferences, it was decided to substitute money that could be identified. A half million in brand new tens, twenties and fifties was secured in exchange for the money Rovere had accumulated. The bills were mechanically and manually aged, shuffled so as to destroy the sequence, then repackaged. It was thought that with such a large amount, it was unlikely that the kidnapers would discover the serial sequence of the bills. The money filled two good-sized suitcases.

Ten days after the kidnaping a letter came to Rovere's office. It had been mailed in Dallas. It was impossible to trace the paper or the envelope. It detailed a plan for transfer of the money that was so clever and so foolproof that it was never leaked to the press. It promised that, after the money was inspected, the boys would be released in a major city. The frustrated police had to permit the transfer of the money. It proceeded without incident, twelve days after the kidnaping. The three tables of serial sequence had been quietly distributed to all banks. Two weeks passed and the boys were not released.

The bodies of the two boys were found a mile from the town of Vanderpool, a little over twenty miles from Rovere's summer place. Both children had been killed by a blow that broke the skull, and they had been placed in a shallow arroyo and carelessly covered with sand and rock. Wind had blown the sand and uncovered the feet of one of the children, and an Angora goat herder had discovered the cairn. It was then that the crime exploded in the papers, complete with all known details except the serial sequence of the money.

The money began to turn up in the banks of Youngstown, Ohio. It was traced to a young man who drove a pickup with Pennsylvania plates. He had rented a small farmhouse near Orangeville, just over the Pennsylvania line. The farmhouse was surrounded, and there was a gun battle during which one officer was seriously wounded and the three occupants of the farmhouse were slain: a young man, an older man, and a young woman. They all had police records. The young man and the young woman were known drug addicts. A single suitcase containing just over a hundred and sixty-five thousand dollars was brought back to headquarters in Youngstown.

There were conflicting stories about whether or not there had been another suitcase, and, if so, what had happened to it. The story of the serial numbers appeared in the newspapers and over radio and on television. State, county, and city police had co-operated with federal officers in the operation. There were intensive inquiries. The other suitcase, if indeed there had been one, was not traced. Some believed there had been at least one and maybe two other principals involved, and that the group had split up. Others thought a cop had grabbed the rest of the money. If others were involved, they would have learned they could not spend the money.

Paul Verney had not been thinking of that money when he was contacted by a man named Roger Dixon. He had known Dixon in law school, had known him quite well in fact, but had lost touch with him after graduation. Dixon had gone into criminal law in Detroit and had been very successful until, in 1949, he was tried and convicted of bribery of a city official, fined, given a suspended sentence and disbarred. Verney had read of the incident and was astonished at Dixon's carelessness.

It was about two months after Catton's heart attack that Paul Verney returned one evening from his office to the private club where he lived and found Roger Dixon waiting for him. Dixon looked prosperous, confident and sleek. He came up to Verney's room to talk to him.

Verney's room was sedate, old-fashioned and comfortable. Verney fixed him a Scotch. "Old Paul," Dixon said. "You look just like I imagined you'd look. You've fulfilled your early promise. I used to think you must have been born looking like a self-satisfied bachelor. What ever happened to Melissa?"

"We were married. She had a breakdown six years ago. A very tragic and unexpected thing, Roger. She's in an institution down-state. The boy is away at school. He's fifteen."

Verney had expected the usual expression of sympathy. Instead, Dixon grinned at him, a bright malicious grin. "And you love every minute of it, don't you?"

"Exactly what are you trying to say?"

"Just that I know you pretty well. Skip it."

"You're looking very prosperous, Roger."

"You know about my little difficulty. I can see you do. And you're disappointed not to find me on a corner with a tin cup and pencils."

"I'm glad you're getting along."

Dixon smiled in a mocking, unpleasant way. "I'll bet you are. Good old Paul. Wants the best for everybody. Don't try to kid me. You don't care and never have cared what happened to anybody else in the world. I roomed with you, Paul. Maybe nobody else ever got behind that façade, but I did. I don't know what it was that twisted you. It must have happened real early. Because by the time we met, you were solidified."

"I don't have to listen to this."

"But you will, Paul. You will, because I know you're in

73

a hell of a jam and you just squeaked out from under an indictment for fraud, and you have the correct impression that I've come here with some kind of an offer where you can make money. So you just let me tell you what you wouldn't listen to a lot of years ago."

"You were always emotional."

"But you weren't, Paul. Emotions were left out of you. I watched you go after everything you wanted. Cold as a machine. No mercy, no scruples, and no ethics."

"The disbarred attorney gives a lecture on ethics."

"I mean ethics in human relationships. When anything or anybody got in your way, you bulldozed the obstacle aside. I've never seen such cold-hearted, cold-blooded, frightening ambition. You didn't make one friend. I was the poor, warm, stupid slob who tried to be your friend. I even tried to understand you and find out what made you what you were and what you are."

"Shouldn't you be accompanied by violins?"

"I should have caught on quicker. Absolute greed plus perfect selfishness plus a ruthless and methodical intelligence. I should have caught on and stayed away from you. Then you wouldn't have gotten the idea of marrying Melissa. The only reason you wanted her was because I wanted her."

"She made the choice."

"On insufficient data. I've kept track of you, Paul. You were getting money and power just as fast as I expected you to. Maybe a little faster. And then you got clobbered. You tripped up and you went down like a horse on ice. I got pleasantly drunk the night I heard about that, Paul. It was a celebration. I bought drinks for strangers, and I made them all drink to my toast. Here's to the utter ruin of Paul Verney, the blackest-hearted bastard of them all."

"You're still emotional, Roger. You mentioned my methodical intelligence. It causes me to ask a question. You seem to . . . disapprove of me. And you hint of some offer that will bring me a profit. Thus the offer is suspect, isn't it?"

"The direct mind at work. I'm an agent in this matter. When you hear the whole story, you'll see why you're the logical one to come to. You have larceny in your soul, but you've stayed relatively clean. You are desperate, and you've got guts. I'll never deny you that. This is going to take careful planning on your part, and you're capable of that. You can make a couple of hundred thousand tax-free dollars. I make a commission and please my boss. I'd foul you up if I could see a way to do it, but I can't think of a way. You're ideal for this proposition."

Verney folded his pale, powerful hands. "I am listening."

Dixon hitched his chair forward and lowered his voice. "Remember the Rovere case? The money? It's never showed up. It's still too hot. It will always be too hot. Want to know a little history? You can't prove any of this no matter what you decide. There's three hundred and twenty-seven thousand. All of the fifties and all of the twenties. A county cop grabbed it that night, drove three miles with it and pitched it into the brush and recovered it the next morning. He sat on it for nearly a year, scared to spend it, scared to unload it. He sold it for ten thousand he could spend. He sold it so he could sleep nights. A speculator in Cleveland bought it and, after a second thought, was happy to unload it in Detroit to a friend of mine a week later for fifteen. My friend figured to sit on it for a couple of years until the heat went off and he could risk spreading it around. But the heat has never gone off. He needs some money. It's on the market. He'll let it go for eighty."

"Why come to me?"

"It can't be sold in the usual channels. Nobody will touch it. Get caught and it's too hard for people like that to prove they weren't in on the snatch. We had a talk about it a month or so ago. I had a few ideas. One of them was you."

"What good would that money do me?"

"You're clean. So is Catton. But you're both larcenous types. You can get it out of the country. Hell, either of you can take all the trips you want. Take it out in small chunks. You two can even keep it in a safety deposit box. South America, Central America, Mexico. You can trade it there. Suppose you hit five or six banks in Rio. Convert it and then convert it back. Months later the stuff drifts

75

back into the Federal Reserve System. By then it's too late to identify where it came from."

"So why don't you do it?"

"Because there is some strange difficulty about getting a passport. And I have no legitimate business reason for a trip. You and Catton have stock in a Panamanian shipping line and in two small South American air lines."

"How the hell would you know that?"

"Paul, I think that's the first time I ever heard you say a naughty word. Never mind how I know."

"The stock is practically worthless."

"But you've got it."

"Can't any of your ... associates get out of the country?"

"There is a kind of unreasoning, superstitious dread about this money, Paul. It doesn't make sense, but it's there. My friend, the guy who wants to sell it, was in France three months ago. He took fifty thousand of it along and lost his nerve and brought it all back and put the whole bundle in what he considers a safer place. I think you're too hardheaded to be superstitious about it."

"What do you get out of this?"

"Ten per cent."

"Why doesn't he take the whole bundle and leave for good, go some place where he can't be sent back?"

"He's a patriot. He likes milk shakes and air conditioning. And he's got other irons in the fire. Is Luciano happy?"

"I'll ... I'll have to think."

"You can't miss. Can you raise the money?"

"Not now. Not the way things are. Maybe the two of us can, if Catton will go for it."

"He'll go for it, if he's as smart as you are, Paul. It's what I told my friend a month ago. It's got to be sold to somebody legitimate. It's too risky to try to do anything with it here. You might pass three thousand bucks before some smart teller checks the list. Once that starts, you wouldn't hear about it. They'd just close in on you, using every bill as a signpost, like a paper chase."

"How do I get in touch with you?"

"I'm registered at the Hancock House. I'll wait."

76

"How can I be sure it's the money? This would be a fine way to unload counterfeit."

Dixon grinned merrily. "Why, if you have any doubts, take one of those fifties to the bank and ask about it, pal."

"But . . ."

"It's legitimate. I'll give you a clipping with those three sets of serial numbers and you can check. It's the money. You'll be buying three dollars for . . . no, four dollars for every one."

Catton, lying listless and wasted in bed, had been frightened by the idea. It had taken Paul two hours to convince him. By the time he left, Burt Catton was exhausted. And Paul knew just how far they could go. Forty from Burt and twenty-five from him would strip them almost completely. Sixty-five thousand.

He offered Dixon sixty. Dixon was amused, indignant, enraged. Paul stood firm. Dixon left and made a phone call. He came back and said seventy was rock bottom. Paul offered sixty-five and said it was absolute top. Dixon was gone much longer the second time. He came back and said, "All right. It's fine. It's just dandy. I don't get ten per cent. I get five per cent. Instead of eight grand I get a lousy three and a quarter, so he only nets one and a quarter less than if you took it at seven. The rest of the difference comes out of my hide. Write this down. Ready? Hogan 68681. That's a Tulsa exchange. Phone any day next week in person, from Tulsa. Ask for Jerry. Have the sixty-five with you in cash. No thousands. When you get Jerry on the line ask him if he knows where you can buy a good used Cad. He'll take it from there."

"Tulsa!"

"It's a city. Like in Oklahoma. You won't like it. Few people do."

And as they had parted then, the last time Verney had seen Dixon, Roger had looked at him intently and curiously and said, "It must have really been something."

"What do you mean?"

"When your toy train went off the tracks. The first major setback in your whole life. It must have really

77

rocked you, Paul. Did you chew up the carpets and run around the walls?"

"I was disappointed."

"You were more than that, Paul. You were shocked. The whole world was turned upside down. They couldn't do this to you. Not to the one and only, the unique Paul Verney. Actually. I'm surprised you didn't kill yourself. Or lose your mind. I had high hopes. I figured you far too brittle to adjust to failure. You see, I can remember the times you got crossed up in little ways. Your reaction was murderous."

"Your imagination has always been too vivid, Roger."

Dixon sighed. "I should have known I'd guess bad again. You'll handle this well. You'll make a potful. You'll screw Catton out of his end, and you'll come out right on schedule or ahead, even. I just have one small hope. I hope I never have to look at you again."

"You should be able to arrange that, Roger."

He told no one where he was going. He told his office staff he was going on a fishing trip. Catton, with face like a skull, had managed to totter into the bank and sign for a safety deposit box and carry it into a booth and take out the cash Paul needed. There were no thousand-dollar bills in either reserve fund. It was nearly all in hundreds, with a very few fifties. Verney packed the money in the bottom of his grip, two packets fastened with rubber bands each nearly three inches thick. The night before he left he thought of the money and how all of this might very easily be an intricate confidence game. In the morning he put the money into two cigar boxes and mailed them separately to himself at the Tulsa hotel where he had made a reservation under the name of W. W. Ward, writing on the outside of each package, *Hold for Arrival*.

He reached Tulsa in three days, phoned the hotel, found the packages had arrived and were being held, and he asked they be put in the hotel safe. When he checked in they gave him a receipt for the two packages. He mailed the receipt to himself care of General Delivery at Tulsa. Then, unable to think of any further way to protect himself, he went to a drugstore booth and phoned and asked for Jerry and spoke nonsense about a used car.

He was picked up that night on a dark corner ten blocks from the hotel. He sat in the back seat of a sedan between two men who had no desire to talk. The driver wore a baseball cap and his ears stuck out, silhouetted against oncoming lights as they left the city and drove very fast for a long time. They stopped and the driver got out and opened a cattle gate and drove in and closed the gate and drove another quarter mile to a house. They shut him in a small bare room with the money. It was tightly packed into a cheap dark blue suitcase with a single wide gray stripe. He checked the serial numbers against the clipping Dixon had given him. The money looked good, looked authentic. He made a halfhearted attempt to count it, and estimated it was all there. He knocked and they let him out and he talked in a dark hallway to a stocky man whose face he never saw.

"Satisfied?"

"Yes."

"Where's your end?"

"I can't get it until after nine tomorrow."

"You stay here tonight and I'll send you in and you get it and you'll be brought back out."

"No."

There was an understanding silence. "How do you want to do it?"

"I'll take this in with me. Your people can stay close to me. I'll turn over my money."

"I don't like that."

Verney suddenly had a better idea. "Take me back to the city now. I'll meet you, alone, tomorrow, at ten in the morning, at any busy public place you want to name. We will meet and decide where to make the exchange."

They met in front of a large department store. Verney recognized the suitcase. The stocky man had a broad impassive face, a slightly Indian look. He said, "If you say where, you can have a setup working. Same with me. So where do we go?"

"Let's get a cab."

"No cab stands. The first cruiser. It better come quick. This is making me sweat."

A taxi came by moments later. Verney hailed it and it swung in to the curb. Verney said to the driver, "Where did you take your last fare?"

"Way out on Fernandez. What's the scoop?"

"What's the last public place, big place, you took a fare to?"

"What kinda gag is this? Lessee . . . railroad station."

Verney looked at the stocky man and he nodded. "Take us there, please."

They went to the men's room, rented dim stalls. Verney sat with the suitcase across his knees and opened it. He dug down to be certain it wasn't a thin layer of money. He snapped it shut and walked out, and the voice from the neighboring stall said sharply, "Watch it! Stay right there where I can watch your feet." Verney heard the rustle of paper. He waited a full five minutes, cold sweat trickling out of his armpits. The door opened and the stocky man came out, the two cigar boxes under his arm, clamped tightly against him. Verney expected some comment. The man gave a single abrupt nod and left. Verney followed him quickly, but stayed fifty feet behind. When he saw the man shut himself into a phone booth on the far side of the station, he walked quickly out and found a cab and directed him to take him to the hotel garage. He locked the suitcase in the back of the Dodge and drove the car around and parked it in the front. Ten minutes later he was on his way out of town. He was unable to take a really deep breath until he was through Bartlesville on Route 75 north. He felt as though he had handled himself very well indeed. There was three hundred and twenty-seven thousand dollars in the trunk of the car. Catton, despite the fact he had put up forty of the sixty-five, had agreed to an even split.

They took the calculated risk of putting the money in safety deposit boxes. Once again Catton was driven down to the Hancock Bank and Trust. They shut themselves into one of the larger cubicles and made a careful count of the money. Catton wanted an even division, each man holding onto his share.

"You had better let me hold it all, Burt."

"No thank you."

"Use your head, will you? You are coming along fine. But you have had a coronary. It's possible you could have another. Then the court opens your boxes. Where will that leave me?"

"If we do it your way and if I should . . . have bad luck, Paul, it will be your good luck, won't it?"

"That is an unkind thing to say."

"We'll do it my way, Paul. That will give you a good reason to move as fast as you can on this matter."

And Verney was not able to change his mind. It was agreed that Paul would take an extended trip in November and December, taking fifty thousand from each share and handling the conversion and reconversion of funds in five South American countries. The monies so obtained would be used as partial payments on the tax indebtedness in January. Paul would set up a dummy transfer of real estate holdings to account for the cash in hand. By that time Catton would be able to travel, and would convert an equal amount. The following summer Paul would convert the balance. By fall all tax claims would be satisfied and there would be a small but comfortable surplus for each of them. Too careful an investigation of the dummy real estate transfers would cause embarrassing questions about where the funds had come from, but it was a chance they felt worth taking. With Paul hitting South America, then Catton hitting Central America, then Paul disposing of the balance on the continent, it was likely that they would stay a long jump ahead of any investigation once the identity of the money was discovered. With both boldness and careful planning, it could be done.

Verney parked his car in the shed garage behind the Center Club, went in the back way, and took the front elevator up to the third floor to his room. All the way back from the camp he had been disturbed because he could not think with the clarity and purpose and method that was so much a part of his nature. He knew that apprehension had given an emotional coloring to his mental processes. Bronson's tough, knowing face kept intruding.

He prepared himself for thought, for the cold evaluations he depended upon. He put on a worn flannel smoking jacket and sat in the deep leather chair half turned toward the double window. The sky over the city was overcast; the light that came into the room was gray.

The loose mouth of a sick man. The unfortunate choice the sick man's wife had made in a partner in her sexual adventures. The career and reputation of Bronson. Catton's precarious health. Seven years Bronson owed the state. The written report that was Bronson's insurance. These were factors. He examined each one, holding each factor up in turn to examine its texture and its curious shape. There would be a way one would fit against another, and a way to slide a third in place. And in the end there would be a picture, one that he could accept.

Primary assumption: The danger of the situation might very well kill Catton. Any logical development of the situation might kill him. First step: Get the money out of Catton's safety deposit boxes. But Catton would have to be given a milder reason. Yet a logical one.

Tell Catton there was too much chance the boxes might be opened by court order. Explain constant worry about that eventuality. Say it would be far better to remove the money to a place not only safer but more accessible. Such as the office of Paul Verney.

He decided that could be done, and should be done tomorrow.

Then, with all funds accessible to him, he could pay Bronson the two hundred thousand. If there was no other answer.

If there was an answer, it would depend on an unknown third person, the one who held the written statement Bronson had prepared. What sort of person? Considering Bronson's background and record, it was unlikely it was a bank or attorney. A close contact. A trusted individual. Bronson would have to be reasonably certain that the one he trusted would not open the envelope, would not learn the actual dimensions of blackmail. He would be unlikely to trust any criminal. And an honest man would not be

82

likely to trust Bronson to the extent that, by holding the envelope, he might become involved in one of Bronson's schemes. It was logical there would be some other hold. A relative? A woman?

A woman. Though it was pure assumption the idea had the proper ring. Bronson was a type to keep a woman cowed and obedient. That added to the danger. Should something happen to Bronson, she was likely to do exactly as he had directed.

Were there any possible ways of finding out who the person was? Following Bronson was impossible. Trying to backtrack him was unfeasible. Who would know his contacts? Bronson had labeled himself a parole violator. He was wanted. Someone would be making an active investigation, attempting to locate him. Could Bronson be made to talk? Not likely. Very little weakness in him. Get back to the parole officer.

It would be logical to assume that the parole officer would know Bronson's contacts—would have them watched. Would it be possible to get information from such a man? Perhaps, with the proper lie, the logical and convincing story. He remembered that Marian would have Bronson's name on the appointment book as of last Thursday morning.

Where is this heading? Suppose it is possible to find Bronson's contact, and possible to retrieve the envelope.

The only way Bronson could be kept from protecting himself would be to kill him.

This was, then, the last fragment of the puzzle. He looked at it, at the shape of it, trying to see if it would fit. The camp was isolated. Bronson was strong and quick and sly. There was very little time. It might be possible to stall him, but not for long. He wanted the money Wednesday afternoon. Seventy-two hours.

The alternative was poverty and disgrace.

He tried to stand off to one side and look objectively at himself and determine whether he was capable of taking a life. It made his hands feel chilled. Yet there were certain rationalizations. Bronson was a criminal, a wanted man— of no benefit to society, only expense. Surely the investigation of such a death would be half hearted. It would be thought he had been slain by one of his own kind. If risk were the only consideration, Bronson was a feasible victim. The greatest risk would be in that he looked to be a man difficult to kill. Yet, depending on his insurance, Bronson would be off guard.

And it would only be possible if the insurance was no longer valid, and if Bronson was not aware of that.

He knew that this was a very involved and intricate situation. Yet there was one favorable aspect to it. The most dangerous and irrevocable step came at the very end. The other steps could be attempted. If there was no possibility of finding the envelope, of learning who held it for Bronson, then the only recourse would be to pay Bronson what he asked. But if the written statement could be found and destroyed, then Bronson could be destroyed.

He checked back over his reasoning. Would it be worth the chance to kill Bronson without finding the statement first? Only if it was a fair gamble that, upon learning of Bronson's death, the holder of the statement would read it and try to use it for profit . . . and be handled in turn.

First things first. Move quickly, but carefully, and plan as you go. One step provides balance and footing for the next.

On Monday morning, after a long conversation with Burt Catton, the money was removed from the safety deposit boxes and transferred to Paul Verney's office safe.

It was eleven-thirty before Paul Verney learned that Daniel Bronson was responsible to a parole officer named John Keefler. He left word for Keefler to phone him. Keefler called back a few minutes after noon, and said that he was free to stop by and see Mr. Verney at two.

CHAPTER SIX

John Keefler

Keefler had sauerkraut and franks at Mel Stodd's Courthouse Restaurant, and as he ate he looked around for someone who might know the score on Paul Verney, the man he had to see at two o'clock. Verney had mystified Keefler by mentioning Danny Bronson.

The restaurant was thick with smoke and the rumble of conversation. Keefler knew more than half the customers—county and city cops, newspaper people, politicians, courthouse types. Sometimes he ate at one of the big tables with a bunch of them, listening, contributing nothing. Usually he ate alone at one of the small tables against the wall opposite the long bar. It did not bother him that he was never greeted as so many of the others were, with wide grins, coarse jokes, and a thumb on the shoulder. He had never tried to win any popularity contests. He thought such actions artificial and ridiculous.

He was nearly finished when a man he knew fairly well came in, a red-faced man in his early fifties named Will Slater. Will had started out as a cop, had quickly achieved detective status, and had studied law at night school. He had been transferred to the Special Detail working under the jurisdiction of the D.A. and later, when he had passed his bar, he had resigned from the force and been taken on as an assistant D.A., a position he had held for over ten years despite a change in administration. He apparently had no desire to enter private practice.

Slater stopped at the bar and Keefler went up and tapped him on the shoulder. Slater turned, his grin fading slightly, and said, "What's on your mind, Johnny?"

"Spare a minute?"

Will told his friends he'd be right back and he went over to the small table, bringing his big stein of black beer along.

"One of the guys I got the file on is on the run, Will. Danny Bronson. Name mean anything?"

"Not a hell of a lot. One of Kennedy's boys. Husky blond, isn't he?"

"That's the one. Quit his job and give up his room and took off. I got a pick-up out on him. None of them are going to fool around with Johnny Keefler."

Will Slater looked at him somberly. "I hear things here and there, Johnny. Maybe you don't remember you're not a cop any more."

"I got a book. It's got the rules in it. Anyway, here's what I want to ask. I get a call from a lawyer. I got to see him at two. He says it's about Bronson. His name is Paul Verney. You know him?"

Slater frowned slightly. "I know him. Not well. He's a very smooth article. For a while he was nearly out of the law game, he was so mixed up in real estate deals. It was Verney and Burt Catton sewed up that big plot of land on options and sold it to Vulcan Aircraft. Now he's doing more law work. He played it too close to the line and the tax boys clipped his wings. He isn't what you could call a shyster. But he's fast on his feet."

"How would he tie in with Danny Bronson?"

"I don't see it. If Danny wanted to make a deal, he wouldn't use Verney as a contact."

"Bronson isn't making any deals. He's going back to Alton."

"Why don't you send them all back, Johnny? They can build a big new wing on the prison. The Keefler wing. And we can all pay more taxes. What you're doing isn't like the cops, Johnny. They can bump you out of that job."

"I'm calling 'em as I see 'em. If they don't like it, I'm not going to cry."

Slater got up, started to say something, then shrugged and said, "See you around, Johnny." He went back to the bar. Keefler saw him say something to his two friends and saw them both look over at him.

By the time Keefler had waited ten minutes in the hushed atmosphere of Verney's tiny waiting room, he had reluctantly come to a higher evaluation of Verney's importance. When the girl told him he could go in he felt much the same sort of unpleasant expectancy as when, in the past, he had been called on the carpet by the head of the division.

Verney was a bigger man than he expected. Big and solemn and remote. His hand was cold and strong.

"I've been trying to figure the tie-in with Danny Bronson," Keefler said as he sat down.

"Bronson made an appointment and came in to see me last Thursday morning, Mr. Keefler."

"Came here! He was in town?"

"He sat in that chair where you are sitting."

"What the hell did he want?"

"He seemed quite furtive. Upset, I would say. I didn't find out until later, of course, that he is a wanted man. Apparently he had picked my name at random out of a phone book. He had some document he wanted me to keep. It was in a sealed envelope. He explained that he wanted me to put it in my office safe and, should anything happen to him—if he should be killed, I believe he meant—I was to turn the envelope over to the police."

"Have you got it? Let me have it!"

"Just a moment, Mr. Keefler. I tried to ask him some questions about himself. I tried to get some idea of the nature of the document I was to hold. He was most evasive. I finally refused to oblige him, even though the fee he offered was generous. I suspected from the way he acted he was involved in something illegal."

"Shakedown!" Keefler said bitterly.

"He said he could find somebody. He was . . . abusive. This morning, just out of curiosity, I phoned the police and found out he is wanted for violation of parole. I was referred to you. I thought it was information you might like to have."

"I sure appreciate it, Mr. Verney. It's something I'm glad to know. Danny has dropped clean out of sight. He quit his job the end of June. I find out he is doing okay. At least he was doing okay in July. But this thing has me stopped. I was a cop until I got hurt. I've been using cop channels. I've had all the boys checking their informants to see if anybody knows anything. I get nothing. He used to be one of Kennedy's boys. He's known all over town. Nobody sees him. Nobody knows what he's doing. He's avoiding every contact. The last time, until I came here, that I could definitely pin him down as being in town was July twenty-fifth. I'd half decided he left for good. A guy with his background, it isn't reasonable nobody would make him. And I couldn't figure out how he could be doing good without my being able to find out how."

"But this gives you a better idea?"

"Yes. It sounds like he's got somebody on the hook, but good. He's milking somebody. Maybe it's a solo flight, and maybe he's got a woman in with him. He could be holed up right here in town."

"Did he contact somebody on the twenty-fifth of July?"

"His brother, Lee Bronson. He called on them and took his brother a birthday present. His brother lives out in Brookton on Arcadia and teaches at Brookton Junior College. I was there Saturday. They haven't seen him since that day he stopped by."

"I don't imagine he'd leave an envelope with his brother, the one he tried to get me to keep?"

"I don't know. Could be. I could go shake them up some, the brother and his wife. Sure, they could have it. That would be a logical place. By God, if that pair lied to me . . ."

"Just a moment, Mr. Keefler. I've remembered something else he said. I guess I should have remembered it before. It might give you a lead. As I told you, he was being abusive. He was shouting at me almost incoherently. He said he had friends who would keep it for him. He mentioned two first names. I don't see how they could be of very much help to you. One name was Fred and the other was, I am quite certain, Tommy."

Keefler sagged in the chair. "No last names?"

"No."

"My God, this is going to mean leg work. Damn! Maybe fifty or sixty guys. I could sit right here and think of fifteen possibles. Great! But I'll have to do it, I guess. It sounds like he was aiming for a big score. It he makes it, he'll be long gone."

After he had thanked Verney again, Keefler went down to Central Records. It took fifteen mintues to get an approval of his request, and another hour to set up the sorter to drop out the punch cards of all local known criminals with the two first names. The sorted cards were run through the tabulator and Keefler was provided with a list of forty-nine names, together with last known addresses. Five were currently serving time and could be eliminated. Keefler checked the names against the yellow sheet files and arbitrarily eliminated eighteen of them as being too young. It seemed logical that Danny would trust older, steadier men. The remaining list of twenty-six names was smaller and more manageable.

Keefler looked forward to the evening with pleasure. His mission was legitimate. He had known some of the men on the list for years. There wasn't one of them who was going to be happy to see him. He would make a little small talk. Hold off until they were uncomfortable. Then set it up just right. What would be a good way?

"Danny Bronson did some talking before he died an hour ago. He said you're holding an envelope for him. Let's have it."

That was a good way. There'd be a reaction—enough so you could tell. Enough to go to work on. It was as good as being a cop. In some ways it was better. In some ways it was even a lot better.

CHAPTER SEVEN

Lucille Bronson

Tuesday was a day of gray and dismal rain, and Lucille felt that her whole life ahead of her was as dreary as the skies. She had awakened when she heard the familiar sound of Lee backing the car out of the drive. She had turned over and tried to go back to sleep but she could not. She kept thinking of how grim and unfriendly Lee had been ever since he had found out about the money and taken it away from her. He had not touched her or kissed her. He had looked through her, as if she weren't there.

She sat on the edge of her bed and stretched and yawned and then reached up under the old pajama top of Lee's that she slept in and gently scratched her round stomach and tousled her hair with the other hand. She looked at the day and grunted with distaste and boredom. Sunday was the last day the pool was open. Now it would be closed for the winter. Damn the long miserable winter. She liked the feel of hot sun on her body. She liked the dazed laziness, the feeling of softness and content, half asleep with Ruthie propped beside her, droning away, talking, talking.

Maybe Lee would let her get a sunlamp. It wouldn't be the same, but it would be something. Ruthie could come over and they could stretch out under it and really get an all over, without any stripes or strap marks or anything.

She trudged into the bathroom, listlessly brushed her hair, cleaned her teeth, put on a fresh mouth. It was too darn much trouble to get dressed on this kind of a day. And there was no point in looking good for Lee. She had come home alone Saturday night after midnight and instead of pacing around worrying about her and bawling

90

her out when she got home, he'd been in bed and asleep.

She got into an aqua corduroy thing that Lee had, during friendlier days, called her battle dress. It was a one-piece garment with short sleeves, knee length legs, a wide belt with a brass buckle, and a zipper from throat to crotch.

Lee had rinsed his breakfast dishes and put them in the sink. She turned on the gas under the coffee, put bread in the toaster, and reassembled the morning paper. She finished the paper before her second cup of coffee was finished. It had started to rain again. She looked vacantly at the counter top, looked without focus at the row of canisters, and then focused on the largest one— and felt a curious shiver start deep inside her and run all the way up into her throat and leave her slightly breathless.

Why not?

Danny was responsible for the way Lee was acting. Danny had put her in the dog house. And Danny, acting like a crazy animal of some kind, had made her submit to him—had really made her unfaithful to Lee. She would never have been unfaithful to Lee, never in this world, if Danny hadn't beat her up and cut her mouth and made her do it. She'd been too scared to scream, even.

Ruthie knew she wasn't like that at all. Ruthie would know on account of Lew. Of course, Lew was only nineteen, just a kid really, but he had that cute grin and those big brown shoulders and he was always at the pool and came over and he always started kidding around, always making a play for her, not for Ruthie. She guessed Ruthie had kinda wanted to make trouble, asking her why she didn't give the kid a break. Go on, Seel. Give him a date. I won't say a word, honest. Lew had a beat-up old car and he wanted her to meet him and they'd go out dancing some night way out of town some place. She had known Ruthie wouldn't say anything, and she knew she could keep Lew in line afterward, even if she did let him do anything, but it wasn't that. It was just she was married and you didn't do that kind of thing. It was all right kidding around with him there by the pool with a lot of people around, but a date was something else. He did get kinda fresh, like the times when she'd be on her

91

stomach and he'd real sneaky run his hand under the big beach towel she was on, and she'd let him go ahead for just a little while, just long enough to feel sort of sweet and dizzy, and then make him cut it out and tell him he could put more oil on her back.

It was Danny's fault, and it was Danny who'd made a real tragic thing happen so all the rest of her life she'd maybe feel a little bit ashamed of herself.

So why not anyway just take it out and look at it?

It began to seem to her that the only thing she could see in the kitchen was the yellow canister with those dumb ducks on it and the fancy printing that said *flour*. When she tried not to look at it her eyes kept swinging back. Suddenly she got up, locked the back door, snatched the canister, took it over to the sink, dug her fingers down into the softness of the flour, felt the edge of the envelope, and pulled it out, tapping it against the edge of the canister to knock the loose flour off of it.

There wasn't any harm in just looking at it.

It was a long white envelope with the gummed flap stuck down and scotch tape pasted over it. She tried to lift a corner of the tape. It came up, but it pulled part of the paper with it. It felt as if there was just one sheet of paper in the envelope. She thought of various ways of opening it. But with the scotch tape there, anything she did would show and Danny would see it, and she was scared of Danny.

Suddenly she had an idea. She trotted into the living room and yanked open the drawer where Lee kept stationery. Yes, he had long white envelopes too. She measured one against the sealed one. It was almost the same—a little bit whiter and a tiny bit longer. The scotch tape on the small roll was the same width.

She stood very still, took a long deep breath, and then ripped the envelope open. She took out the single sheet and unfolded it, held it in tremulous hands and read it. It had been written with a ball-point pen in Danny's rough scrawl.

To whom it may concern,
  Burton Catton and Paul Verney have got the rest of

the Rovere ransom dough. Mrs. Catton told me about it.
Mr. Catton told her. They figure on peddling it outside the
country. They bought it through a Detroit contact, and
Verney picked it up in Tulsa. The Detroit contact is
named Dickson. I am going to try to take it off them and
if anything happens to me it will be one of them arranged
it. Make sure Sarge Ben Wixler gets to read this. He knows
I wouldn't kid about a deal like this.

Daniel A. Bronson

Lucille read it again, confused, incredulous. As an in-
veterate reader of the social columns, she knew of Burton
Catton. He had a young wife. She was a Downey. She
took her maiden name back after something happened to
her first husband. She used to ride show horses. She
didn't know who Paul Verney was. The name had a very
faint familar ring, something to do with a charity drive.
The Red Cross or the Community Chest or something like
that.

She put the sheet in the new envelope, then copied
exactly the way the scotch tape had been put on. She
handled it, bent it, dogeared it until it looked like the
original. She crumpled Danny's envelope, put it in the tiny
untidy fireplace and lighted it. While it was burning she
hurried into the kitchen, buried the envelope in the flour
and replaced the canister. When she went back into the
living room the last bit of flame was flickering out. She
dropped into the biggest chair, curled her legs under her.
Everybody remembered that terrible Rovere thing, those
poor twin kids. Everybody knew about the money. Gee, it
was an awful lot of money. Hundreds of thousands.

Just how could Danny ever get to know Mrs. Catton,
and why in the world would she ever tell him something
like that?

Lucille realized she wasn't bored any more. This was a
big shiny fact. It sat squarely in the middle of her mind,
and it seemed to her that she could walk around and
around it, looking at it from every angle and trying to see
some way it could be grasped and picked up. And used.

She did not doubt that Danny would get the money.
That man was after Danny. They wanted to send him

back to Alton. Danny knew that. When he got the money, he would be able to afford to go a long way away where they couldn't ever get him. Before he went, he would come back after the envelope. When he came back after it, it would mean he already had all that money.

She nibbled her thumb nail, biting it painfully into the quick. She knew that, more than anything else in the world, she wanted to go with Danny. This marriage was a trap, and this stinking little house was a trap. She'd never been meant for this kind of a life. Life was supposed to be gay, and just dangerous enough to be delicious.

She and Danny were on a little terrace outside their hotel suite. You could see the deep blue water of the harbor. Two waiters would roll in the breakfast on a little jingling cart. Maybe one of them would carry an ice bucket with champagne. They'd both be dressed for the private beach.

When the waiters left, Danny would look at her and grin and say, "I must admit you were right, darling." And he had changed some. He looked a little bit like Cary Grant.

"I guess you could call it blackmail," she would say. "You didn't want to bring me with you, but you had to."

And they would laugh and drink the champagne and go down to the beach, and then in the afternoon they would go down a windy little street and into a dark little shop and he would buy her an emerald. They would try not to think of Lee, but when they did they would both feel sad.

There was enough money to last them their whole life.

When Lee came back to lunch, she wanted to laugh the way he looked so surprised at how nice she had made everything.

"What's the occasion?" he asked.

"Does it have to be an occasion? I thought you might like a nice lunch." She couldn't tell him that she was going to do as many nice things as she could for him in the time that was left. Or tell him she hoped there wouldn't be much time left.

After he left and she had cleaned up, she felt restless.

She walked back and forth through the house, snapping her fingers, humming to herself. In the late afternoon the wind increased, the rain stopped and it became colder. She had a long talk with Ruthie over the phone. Ruthie was bored, and Lucille knew she had only to give the slightest hint and Ruthie would come over. But she couldn't see how she could keep from telling Ruthie about everything. It was hard to keep from hinting about it over the phone. So they talked movies and food and television and bargain sales and about what could be causing the stiff neck Ruthie kept getting all the time.

Lee came back from the school at four with a whole stack of papers to go over and he said he had to get right at it because he was going to Dr. Haughton's house after dinner for a conference or something. Dr. Haughton was the head of the English department.

Lee worked in the living room and finished just before dinner. His eyes looked tired and his face looked tired. He did not have much to say during dinner.

After dinner she glanced up and saw that he was staring at her, a curious expression on his face.

"What's wrong with me?" she asked.

"You don't have much fun, do you, Seel?"

"I'm okay."

"The world is so full of a number of things. My God, when I think of how I could use a little more spare time . . ."

"Sure. And I just slop around. I'm not the big brain."

"Let's not fight, please. There's been enough of that lately."

"And it's all been my fault. I know."

"Please, Seel."

"Okay. Okay."

"I've got an idea. I think it would be good for you. They can use somebody in the Bursar's office. Five mornings a week. It wouldn't be hard work. It will pay twenty-five a week. If I should talk to Randy I think . . ."

"Stop thinking, then. If you think I'm going to go there every morning and drudge around, you're completely . . ."

"Okay," he said wearily. "Skip it." He stood up and dropped his balled napkin on the table and looked down

95

at her for a silent moment. "I only thought you might be more contented if you had something to do. You don't seem to have the inclination or the imagination to take up a hobby. I thought it might keep you out of trouble."

"What kind of trouble? Just what do you mean?"

He shrugged. "Who knows what kind of trouble? Maybe I thought it might make this marriage a little better."

"You'd be surprised at how fast it would get better if we didn't have to watch every damn dime. If we didn't have to live in this . . ."

"Shut up!" The explosive violence shocked her. He had leaned toward her to yell at her, his expression savage. For once she had no retort. She heard him get his coat out of the hall closet. He banged the door when he left. She listened to the starter grind and grind until the motor caught. She got up then and began to carry the dishes out to the kitchen.

Who the living hell did he think he was? Who did he think he was yelling at? What right had he to yell? He was the one who sold the big bill of goods. Marry a writer, sure. Teaching was just a hobby. Just temporary. He was scared to write. Look at the money they made writing that junk on television. Thousands and thousands. And him with that one darn book she couldn't hardly read because nothing seemed to happen in it. And those reviews he used to look at but didn't any more. "Sensitive new talent." "Promising young novelist." He'd get to be sixty and they'd retire him with a lousy little state pension and he'd still be the same promising young novelist. He didn't have guts, ambition, drive. So he was going over and lick old Haughton's shoes. Big deal.

She washed the dishes quickly and carelessly and stacked them away, still faintly a-gleam with grease.

When the front doorbell rang, she decided it was Ruthie. Maybe she wanted to take in a movie, or maybe their television was broken again. She flipped off her apron, patted her hair, and walked swiftly through the house. She opened the door. The man was big and lean. The wind flapped his dark topcoat. She looked out at the curb but there was no car there.

"Mrs. Bronson?" His voice was deep and slow and important.

"Yes?"

"I'd like to speak to you a moment. May I come in?"

She hesitated. He wasn't a salesman, she decided. He had the manner of a gentleman. She stepped back and he came into the small hallway.

"Is Mr. Bronson at home?"

"He had to go to a meeting. He left just a little while ago. He probably won't be back for a long time. Is there something I can do?"

He moved from the hall into the living room. She was forced to follow him. It annoyed her that he didn't take off his dark hat. He wore leather gloves. There was something strange about him, about his manner, that made her think that perhaps she had made a mistake in letting him in so readily.

"Can you tell me your name, please?" she asked, and was disturbed that her voice trembled slightly.

"I am doing a favor for a friend. A mutual friend. He asked me to stop by here and pick up something he left here for safe keeping."

He looked down at her. She licked her lips. "I . . . I don't know what you're talking about."

"Yes, you do, Mrs. Bronson. I want the envelope your brother-in-law left here. Get it, please."

"He . . . he sent you?" she asked, and realized at once that she had made a mistake.

"He sent me. He didn't think it was safe for him to come into the city. Get it."

She took two inadvertent steps toward the kitchen and then stopped and turned. He was so close to her that she took a step back away from him. She looked up at him and said, "I can't give it to you. My husband took it and locked it up. I don't know where it is."

He did not answer. He walked toward her. She backed away. He backed her out into the kitchen. "I can't give it to you!" she said thinly.

"Where is it?" he asked. She glanced toward the canisters. She could not help looking toward them. She looked back at him and saw that under his calm look he was excited, he was under great tension. He grabbed her by the arm. The strength of the grip made her gasp with pain. He whirled her over toward the counter, held her against the counter, twisted her arm up between her shoulder-blades. Her forehead hit the cupboards.

"Where is it?" he demanded again. She began to cry. He pushed her away so violently she fell and slid half under the sink. The fall dazed her. She looked up and saw him dumping out the contents of the canisters. Sugar, salt, flour, spilling them on the counter top and on the floor. He took the envelope, ripped it open, glanced at the statement and put it in his pocket. She stood up, holding onto the sink.

"Did he . . . get the money?" she asked weakly.

He turned and looked at her. His expression had changed. "You know about the money," he said softly. "You and your husband know about the money."

"Lee doesn't know . . . " She stopped abruptly as she read the horrid intention in his face. It was unmistakable. She whirled and yanked open the kitchen knife drawer. As she scrabbled at the knife handles, the big leather hand closed on the nape of her neck. She screamed once in fright and pain. He yanked her away, slammed her head down against the gleaming edge of the sink. She felt the sickening impact, felt her skin split over the bone. And then she was far away, and what was happening was a dream, a boneless, fluid, swarming dream in which she sagged against strength and felt herself lifted, then forced down again, slammed down with violence against the white edge of the sink. The impact was a softness, a whirling white like winter snow, and it was like falling into snow, down through cold gray into a deep blue, into a black . . .

CHAPTER EIGHT

Lee Bronson

Dr. Ellis Haughton was a widower who lived
with a married daughter in a modern home on
the western edge of the city. His son-in-law was
a prosperous corporation executive. One wing of the house
had been converted into a compact suite for Dr. Haughton, with kitchen, bath, and private entrance.

Dr. Haughton was a burly old man in his early seventies.
He had headed up the English Department of the State
University at the time of his retirement. With the establish-
ment of Brookton Junior College he had consented to
come out of retirement and take over the job for two
years. The two years had become five. He had been the
man who had interviewed Lee Bronson three years before.

Lee had, at first, wondered why Haughton had been
considered so desirable they had asked him to come out
of retirement. He had seemed a quaint old man, vague,
bumbling, eccentric. He took no classes. He had turned his
neat modern office into a wilderness of papers, notes,
books, disordered files. He had a staff of nine. He seemed
to take no interest in how the instructors, assistant professors, and associate professors organized and conducted
their courses. He was an authority on Chaucer, and every
conversation with him seemed to have a fatal tendency to
drift off into Chaucerian lore. He always seemed to be
a little more than half asleep at faculty meetings.

But slowly Lee came to realize that the carefully hidden
talent, the invaluable talent, was that of the administrator.
Haughton was an expert at the imperceptible nudge.
Somehow each staff member was assigned to that work he
did best and liked most. For some reason his department
was free of the cliques and jealousies that hamstrung other

99

departments. Staff members came up with practical ideas which, when they thought back, had started to germinate after some vague comment by Dr. Haughton. The available scholarships seemed to go to the students who most deserved them. The departmental share of the budget seemed to remain high without any special fuss or energy. And when Haughton came out of his half sleep at faculty meetings, his grumbled comments were highly pertinent and, after argument, were usually adopted.

Lee had asked Haughton if he could see him on a personal matter. Ever since the interview with Keefler, he had worried about the harm Keefler could do him. He had decided to lay it in Haughton's lap, so at least the old man would be forewarned.

The first half hour was given over to a mildly virulent discussion, by Haughton, of a recently published essay on Chaucer written by an instructor at Queen's College who, Haughton said, "has all the organizational ability of a kitten with dysentery."

They sat in two deep leather chairs, half facing the small grate where cannel coal glowed. Haughton sighed and said, "World full of fools. What fool thing have you done, Lee?"

It was difficult to start, but as he went along it became more and more easy to tell Haughton the whole story: the past, the present, and his fear of what could happen in the future. Haughton sat, eyes half closed, thick hands crossed over his belly, fire glint on the lenses of his glasses. When Lee had finished, Haughton was silent. He took off his glasses, huffed on them, cleaned them on the lining of his necktie.

"You like what you are doing, Lee?"

"Why . . . yes. Yes, of course."

"But there is a thing you would like better."

"I . . . I thought so once."

"I read your novel. It interested me. A man writing before he had enough to say. But saying that little bit well. This place, this . . . junior college . . . isn't that a terrible name for a place, a trivial name? . . . it is supported by state funds. That is something to be considered always. The rafters over our heads are full of little termite

100

clerks and experts on the state level. We try to ignore them as much as we can. In times of stress they wave a great banner at you. In great crimson letters it says Taxpayers. We do not have the freedoms of an endowed institution. This Keefler person, if he is as you say he is, and I believe I can trust your judgment about people, could make it impossible for your contract to be renewed. But no matter what he does, I will see that you finish out the academic year."

"Thank you, I . . ."

"It is not entirely a personal thing. You are very good with the young people. And now please do not think for one little moment that I am talking about this insane preoccupation with throwing balls of various shapes and sizes back and forth. That is merely one of the diseases of the era we must endure." He tapped his creased forehead. "The mind. The incredible miracles of intelligence and creative imagination. That is the essence, Lee. These days our young instructors are so crammed with curriculum construction, pedagogical phrases, and modern testing methods they have no time for the development of the mind of the individual pupil. I had a plan of giving you a heavier work load next year, so as to make you give up some of this muscle nonsense. Obviously you have come here for advice."

"Yes."

"It will be blunt. Your brother, in imposing on you, has forfeited his rights to any protection based on silence and sentimentality. Surely this Keefler is not a great and powerful man. If your brother is being hunted, it is a police matter, not a parole matter any longer. I would take that money and I would go to the police. I would go as high as I could get and make a complete statement, and in that statement I would accuse this Keefler of abusing the privileges of his position. He sounds like the sort one must counterattack briskly."

"That makes sense."

"It may be that he will cause trouble anyway. So before he has a chance to cause trouble, I will write to a friend of mine. He has bothered me for years. He thinks I am in this world to be a talent scout for him and for that

101

incredibly dignified institution which employs him. I have sent him two young men in the last ten years. You will definitely receive an offer, written on that superior parchment used for Ivy League communications. Then if it becomes impossible for you here, you can leave gracefully. Even if Keefler can be tamed, perhaps you should leave anyway. Three years here is enough for you, I think. I have one more bit of advice. Also blunt. That pretty little wife of yours might benefit greatly if you were to beat her frequently. I have attempted to converse with her. You would be supplying something her own people obviously neglected. She could have caused you great trouble. She should be made to see the seriousness of that. You have a child wife, and I believe you should face that problem and treat her as a child until she begins to become an adult. If she never changes, you will at least be maintaining control. Now, if you reach far to your right, my young associate, you will find that you can reach the chess set without getting out of your chair. Of the eleven times we have played, you have won three and tied three, and it is your turn to have white, and I consider it highly probable that you will open with that Ruy Lopez again."

As Lee drove home, he felt renewed and confident. Haughton had lightened the strain of the past four days. Not only that, but he had made the future enormously more promising. It was possible, too, that he was right about Lucille. Perhaps he had been wrong in expecting adult reactions from her, when she was not yet ready to give them. She might be happier and feel more secure in a world where she could expect implacable reward and punishment.

He turned into the drive, seeing that the lights were on in living room and kitchen, and not on in the bedroom. He eased the car into the narrow old garage, turned off the weary motor. Halfway between the garage and the house, he stopped and looked up at the night sky. A sliver of moon sailed rapidly through the clouds, and here and there a patch of stars showed. The air was cool and damp. Haughton was an old fox. He had built up a pawn structure that had severely constricted the movements of

Lee's pieces. Haughton, grunting with satisfaction, had slowly strangled him to death, and then had slanted in with the two bishops and forced the checkmate. He grinned and shook his head and went lightly up the back steps.

He was halfway through the kitchen when he saw the spilled canisters. He stopped, puzzled. Then he turned slightly and saw her. She lay on the linoleum in front of the sink, half on her side, cheek against the floor, one arm folded under her, one leg sharply bent. The dark puddle of blood under her head had reached to the sleeve of her outflung arm, had soaked into the aqua corduroy. He did not know how long he stood there. He felt as if he stood with heart and breathing stopped. He went to her, went down on one knee, touched her shoulder. There was no warmth. Her resilient flesh was not cold. It just had no temperature. The touch sickened him. He bent down and he could see a portion of the ruin of her face. He stood up quickly and gagged and put his fist to his mouth and bit hard on his knuckle.

Dead child. No more to be punished or loved. There was a pink smear of blood on the edge of the sink and the enamel was freshly chipped. He looked at the canisters. Somebody had been looking for something. Danny had come after his money.

He went to the phone, almost on tiptoe. He looked up the police emergency number in the front of the book, dialed it.

"Police Headquarters, Sergeant Foltz."

"This is Lee Bronson of 1024 Arcadia Street, Brookton. Somebody has killed my wife." The words, spoken so carefully, sounded insane.

"Don't touch anything, Mr. Bronson. If there's anybody with you, don't let them leave. Officers will be there in a few moments."

Lee hung up. He stood by the phone. The house was very still. He heard the refrigerator go on. He heard the hiss of bus brakes. Then he heard the thin, oncoming whine of a siren, and he stood without moving until he heard the sound drop to a low growling, and saw the sweep of the spotlight as they picked up house numbers.

He turned on the porch lights and opened the door. Two uniformed men came swiftly up the walk and up the steps. One was young and thin and the other was older, short and wide.

"Bronson? Where is it?"

"In . . . the kitchen. I'd just come home, just a couple of minutes ago, and . . ."

"Save it, Mr. Bronson. They'll be coming along to ask you questions in a couple minutes. Take a look, Billy."

The young one walked heavily through the house. He came back quickly. "No question about this one."

"You stay with Mr. Bronson. I'll confirm." The wide man trotted out to the car.

"Confirm?" Lee said weakly.

"You get some funny calls sometimes. Maybe somebody faints. Maybe somebody's got a knot on the head. That your wife?"

"Yes."

"Rough deal, mister."

"Can I sit down?"

"You better just stay right here. They won't want nothing messed up in the house. They'll be along any minute. A whole swarm of them. Homicide Section and lab guys and the coroner and D.A. office guys and the newspapers. You won't be lonesome." He took two steps out onto the unscreened part of the porch and yelled, "All right, there. Move along. Nothing to see. Move along. Go on back home. Nothing to see, folks."

CHAPTER NINE

Ben Wixler

Sergeant Ben Wixler had worked from eight-thirty to five on Tuesday, the sixteenth of October, and had been driven home by one of the boul cars on the four to twelve which had brought in an early and, for Ben, an opportune D and D they had netted out in his usually circumspect neighborhood. Though he knew that as the acting head of a section he could order up a department sedan and driver, it always made him feel too much as though he was swinging his weight around. It might be different when he made lieutenant, a boost that Matthews had told him was coming up any day now.

The boys let him off in front of his house and as Ben got out he saw Beth looking out the picture window in front. It was a smallish house on a generous lot—a lot that matched the size of the mortgage. Even on such a dismal day the house looked inviting. He'd been very dubious about Beth's idea of painting it barn red with white trim. He had favored white with green trim. But she had won and he had to admit it looked fine. The outside finish was board and batten, and the stubby chimney was painted white.

She opened the front door for him, her pretty face a mock mask of woe, and said, "And there's the police bringing your poor father home again, children."

He kissed her and touched the front of her smock very lightly and said, "Children, indeed! And have you no restraint, woman? If I haven't lost count, and some days I'm not sure if I haven't, that will be number four you're a-carrying. Where are the other monsters?"

"Captivated by television. The same old western. The one they show over and over again."

105

"Then there's no use trying to say hello to them yet." He hung his coat and hat in the hallway closet and went into the living room. By parental decree the television set had been relegated to the play room in the cellar. Sounds of six-shooters drifted up through the floor.

"I must say," Beth said, "I could get to like these banker's hours."

"Don't get too used to them. Things are too quiet. Everything will happen at once. I might as well enjoy it while I can."

"Are you in a good mood? A wonderful mood?"

He scowled at her. "Bash a fender? No. We going out? No." He looked around the living room. "Hmmm. Somebody's coming. Oh, my God! That brother of yours!"

Beth perched on the arm of the chair and ran her fingertips through his hair. It was very short black hair, stiff as wire, fitted like a dense black cap to the round hard skull. "Mmmm," she said. "All scratchy."

"Don't try to soothe me, woman."

"Hank is my brother."

"I grant that."

"Hank is a noisy oaf. Hank patronizes you. Hank asks you questions and doesn't listen to the answer. His darling wife, Eleanor, has all the elfin charm of a coal chute. But, beloved, Hank *is* my brother."

"A highly implausible relationship. Hi ho. I can endure it. My face will grow stiff from wearing a horrid grin. I will applaud his triumphs in the lumber business. And I shall keep one pointed ear canted in the direction of the telephone." He swiveled around to look up at her. "But I swear to God, honey, if he gets off again on that business about maybe I ought to grow up and stop playing cops and robbers and he has a nice opening for me, I'm going to run him right out into the street."

"I don't think he'll try that again. Not after the last time," she said, and giggled. "Anyway, it isn't for dinner this time. They're coming about eight-thirty, and they'll be gone by midnight. Three and a half hours. Now go make like a water buffalo, darling."

He went into the bedroom and undressed for a shower. He had treated Hank's attitude lightly while talking to

106

Beth, but he knew that she guessed how much it disturbed him. Hank's attitude was far too symptomatic to be comfortable. To too many people the job of a cop was without honor, particularly in the city of Hancock where, over the years, too much publicity had been given to the corrupt police officer—and where the police force had had to make a continual compromise with a strong underworld organization.

Hank would never know what it was like.

Ben Wixler had left college in 1942 at the end of his junior year to enlist in the army. At the end of basic training he had almost inevitably been selected to go to O.C.S., and he had elected the infantry school. At twenty-one he had been much the same sort of man he was at thirty-five. Big, solid, impassive and reliable, a man who in ways unknown to himself could generate loyalty and respect. He could, when faced with incompetence or lethargy, became frighteningly cold and ominous, face expressionless, only the gray eyes alive, shining like broken metal. To those close to him he was able to show a wonderful warmth, an understanding generosity. He was often afraid, but he could control it. By '44 he was a captain and had his own company. Company B was the one selected for the nasty jobs, such as the clearing of snipers from small shattered towns, the jobs requiring a high order of discipline, a professional regard for risk. Every man in B Company bitched heartily about the assignments given them, but had a high secret pride in the company and in the steady competence and unrelenting fairness of Wixler. Replacements quickly absorbed this special feeling, and the mortality rate of replacements was the lowest in the division.

Ben Wixler turned down a chance to remain in the army after VJ day, and was discharged with appropriate medals and recognition and a separation promotion to Major. He went back to Hancock in November of 1945, intending to re-enter college for his final year at mid-semester. His father was an officer and director of the Hancock Bank and Trust Company, and it had been Ben's previous plan to finish his Business Administration course, get his degree, and go into the bank. He had not been awfully enthused by that program, even before the war. The years of command and responsibility made the prospect quite tasteless. He was very restless during his terminal leave, moody, drinking too much, dissatisfied with himself, and wondering if he would have done better to stay in.

His father, a man of much perception, introduced him at that critical juncture to Hank Striker, the Chief of Police. Ben's father was one of the few men of prominence in the city who understood the dimensions of Striker's problem, and respected his approach to it. They were close friends. Striker was impressed by Ben Wixler. Striker felt that one day, somehow, the strength of the Bouchards and the Kennedys would be smashed in Hancock. One day they would be stripped of the political power that made it necessary for the police force to embrace expediency rather than efficiency. If that day were to be hastened, and if the force were to be able to handle it when it did arrive, it was necessary to attract to the force now those young men of high purpose and intelligence exemplified by Ben Wixler.

Striker talked to Ben. He talked to him privately and at length and with utter frankness. He told him of the social disapproval he could expect, of the disappointments that would be his. And he lit a fire that did not go out. Wixler changed his major and finished in two years at Northwestern, and did clerical work at Hancock Police Headquarters during the summers. After graduation he was taken on as a rookie, received one citation during that period, and became a patrolman at the end of his probationary period. For the excellence of his work he was made detective after eleven months as a patrolman, and was reassigned to the Homicide Section, headed by Captain Roeber. He knew the extent of his good fortune in the assignment to Homicide. Of all the operating sections, that was the one least subject to outside influence. All other crimes and violations were subject to the fix. Not murder.

In 1950, six months after the death of Striker, and one month before the birth of their first child, Ben Wixler made sergeant. Beth was exactly right for him. It was the best of marriages. He was twenty-nine when they married, and she was twenty-one, a small girl with dark auburn hair and the complexion of a brunette. Her father, a prosperous building supply merchant, deplored the marriage. In addition to their happiness, there was one other factor which, though Ben resented it slightly at first, he later came to realize was most fortunate. Beth, by the terms of her grandfather's will, came into a small inheritance when she was twenty-one. It provided an income of just under eleven hundred dollars a year. Once he was adjusted to that, he told her there should be an unlimited supply of lovely redheads with eleven hundred a year. And they should be reserved for the cops. It provided just enough cushion to make the meager wage palatable.

Soon the promotion to lieutenant would come along. It was inevitable that it should. At the time he had been assigned to Homicide, Captain Roeber had been tough, alert and competent, fully capable of running his section. But during the past two years there had been an unfortunate disintegration of the man, an early and progressive hardening of the arteries of the brain resulting in premature senility. Roeber had become erratic, confused, subject to curious emotional fixations and delusions of persecution.

As that had progressed, the burden of the section had fallen more heavily on the shoulders of the assistant section head, Lieutenant Gabby Grey, and on Ben Wixler. Gabby Grey was a frail reed indeed. He was nearly sixty, a political appointee of forty years ago, nephew of a mayor dead a quarter of a century. When Roeber had been his competent self, there was no burden on Gabby Grey. But with Roeber incapacitated, Gabby could not handle the section. He fluttered, jittered, perspired, and passed the buck to Wixler on nearly every decision.

The new chief was, fortunately, a man from the same mold as Striker. His name was James Purvis, a small, cold, brilliant, dictatorial man. When the confusion in the Homicide Section was pointed out to him, his investigation was quick and thorough. There were many ways it could have been handled, other men who could have been transferred in. But one of Purvis's most valued possessions

109

was the small private notebook kept by Striker, with his personal evaluation of all officers on the force. After checking the notebook, Purvis moved swiftly. He put Roeber on sick leave for the four months remaining before his retirement. He reassigned Gabby Grey to Central Records where it seemed that he could do the least harm. He made Ben Wixler acting head of the Homicide Section, and released Inspector Wendell Matthews from some of his other duties so that he could keep closer check on the performance of the section. All this had happened six months ago, and Ben had been assured that when his promotion came through he would be made head of the section. Until that time he had to move very gingerly insofar as personnel changes were concerned. He knew the ones he wanted to get rid of, and he also knew the young ones he wanted to bring in.

By twenty minutes of twelve that evening Ben had stifled so many yawns his jaw ached. Hank was in the middle of telling, in excruciating detail, the big addition he had made to his yard for the do-it-yourself addicts when the phone rang. Ben reached the hallway phone in five long strides and caught it at the end of the second ring.

"Wixler."

"Cullin, Ben. We got one. Housewife in Brookton. Means is on the way. He ought to be there in three, four minutes."

"Thanks, Shorty."

He went back into the living room. "Sorry, people. I've got to go to work." Beth gave a familiar sigh of resignation.

Eleanor said, "We should be going now anyway. I'm certainly grateful Hank keeps regular hours."

"It's so nice for you, dear," Beth said.

Ben went to the bedroom, picked up gun and badge, then scooped coat and hat from the front hall closet, said good night, kissed Beth, and, as he went down the front steps, saw the sedan glide to a stop at the end of his walk. He ran the rest of the way, and the sedan started up again as he pulled the rear door shut. Detective Dan Means

110

was in the back seat. Detective Al Spence was in the front beside the driver.

There was no time wasted in greetings. "Ten twenty-four Arcadia. Mrs. Lee Bronson. The husband phoned it in. Car 18 checked and confirmed. Looks like she was beaten to death in the kitchen."

"Nice," Ben said dryly. "How are we on schedule?"

"Got the original call at eleven twenty-eight, confirmed at eleven thirty-four. We ought to hit there about the same time as the lab truck."

Ben leaned back in his seat. He knew the most probable pattern. Some heavy drinking, a family quarrel, a drunken blow that hit too hard. He hoped there weren't any kids. That always made it worse. There would be a repentant slob, suddenly sober, too late sober, tearing his hair and bellowing of his great sorrow, his terrible loss. How could he have done such a thing. And with luck Ben thought he could be in bed by one o'clock.

"Party at your house?" Dan asked.

"Just my brother-in-law."

"He offer you a job again?"

"Not this time."

"Maybe you ought to take it, Ben."

Al Spence turned around, arm hooked over the back of the seat. "Ask him for one for me too, Sarge. Something interesting. Like counting boards or driving a lumber truck."

"Looks like it up there in the next block on the right," Ben said. There were four vehicles parked in front of the house, two of them prowls. The porch lights were on. Curious neighbors had gathered, some of them in bath robes. A uniformed officer was moving them back, clearing the sidewalk in front of the house. Just as Ben got out, the lab truck, a converted panel delivery, pulled up. He waited to check the crew, and Catelli came up to him and he saw Roamer opening the back door of the truck. "Who else you got, Catelli?"

"Frenchie's coming in his own car. He ought to be here."

"Get your stuff up on the porch and hold it while I take a look."

111

More than half the front porch was screened. Ben recognized the short, wide officer standing beside a tall, fit, good-looking young man who wore a topcoat and carried a hat in his hand.

"Hello, Tormey."

"Hi, Ben. This here is Bronson. It's his wife. She's in the kitchen." Ben looked at Bronson. He looked sober and shocked.

"My name is Wixler," he said. "I'm in charge. You reported this?"

"Yes, sir. I came home and came through the back way, and ..."

"Drive home?"

"Yes, sir."

"How long ago?"

Bronson looked at his watch. "I must have got here pretty close to eleven-thirty."

Ben nodded at Al Spence and Spence went around the side of the house. There was no need for a specific order. Spence would check the automobile, feel the heat of block, radiator, and tail pipe and make a very accurate estimate of the time of Bronson's arrival.

"Where were you?"

"With the head of the English Department at Brookton Junior College. I'm an instructor there. I was with Dr. Haughton at his home."

"What time did you leave here?"

"At about seven-thirty, maybe a couple of minutes earlier or later. It takes about a half hour to drive over there. I left him at just about eleven, maybe a couple of minutes before eleven."

"Your wife was alone?"

"Yes."

"Did she expect anybody?"

"She didn't say anything about anybody coming here."

Wixler had managed, imperceptibly, to move close enough to Bronson to be assured the man had not been drinking. There was something about Bronson that puzzled him—something he could not quite put his finger on. The man seemed authentically dazed by what had happened. It was a reaction almost impossible to fake. Wixler,

112

in all his investigations, placed considerable credence on his own hunches. He respected the acuity of the workings of the subconscious mind, and his own reactions had been refined by long experience. Until other factors could be added to the mixture, he was content to proceed on the basis that this was a decent man, troubled and hurt.

A man came part way up the steps and said, "How's chance of a shot of the body, Benjamin?"

Wixler turned and looked at Billy Sullivan, at the young-old handsomeness and innocence of the choirboy face, at the unlikely dapperness of this enormously capable crime reporter for the *Hancock Ledger*, the largest of the city's three morning papers.

"You know better than that, Billy," Ben said sadly.

Al came back up the steps and said in an undertone to Ben, "Okay." And Ben knew the car had backed up Bronson's statement. The lab men brought their equipment up onto the porch. Ben looked warily at Sullivan and said to Tormey, "You and Mr. Bronson wait in the hall."

Wixler, Spence, and Means walked into the house. Wixler moved slowly, hands in the slash pockets of his tweed topcoat. Spence and Means stayed a half step behind. Wixler judged the flavor of the living room. A rental, with rented furniture supplemented by Bronson belongings. Many more books than customary. Two good framed reproductions. Indifferent housekeeping, with dust coils under the couch, litter in the small fireplace. They walked on out into the kitchen. He looked at the spilled staples for a long time. He could see the shadow pattern of footprints where someone had stood as the items had spilled.

"Make that, Dan?" he asked.

"A man stood there, wouldn't you say? Looking for something. Those were dumped on purpose."

"No sign of any search in the living room," Al said.

"So," Ben said, "he either found it where he was looking, or he got scared and took off."

"He'll have flour and stuff on his shoes and his clothes," Dan said.

They started to move toward the body. Ben pointed at

the flour on the floor and they stayed back. Ben sat on his heels, bent low to see as much as he could of her face. He grunted with distaste and stood up.

"She was a dish," Al said reverently.

"Go get Catelli and his people. I want pictures, and I want to see if they can get any kind of molds of those footprints before the doctor gets near her."

Wixler, Spence, and Means stood aside while Catelli, Roamer, and Duchesne worked. No mold could be taken. Detailed pictures of the footprints were taken, with a ruler laid beside them. The doctor from the Coroner's Office arrived, a sallow young man who looked bored and overworked. After the position of the body had been chalked out, it was lifted gently at Ben's direction to see if there was any flour under it. There was enough to help him in his reconstruction. The doctor studied the woman's face, tested the armpit temperature, gently flexed the joints of elbow and wrist. Squatting, he looked up at Ben and said, "Roughly about four hours. Quarter after twelve now. So I'll say between quarter of eight and quarter of nine. I don't think we'll pin it down much closer when we take a better look unless you can give me the exact time of the last intake of food. Cause of death I would say so far is due to repeated heavy blows in the facial area resulting in multiple skull fractures. I can see at least three that would have killed her." He stood up.

"Could she have been slammed against the edge of the sink?"

The doctor looked at the sink. "Yes. The shape of the wounds would fit. There would be enough . . . inertia, so that it would have to be a pretty powerful man. After the first blow she would have been unconscious. Her weight would have had to be supported."

"Can you work on her tonight?"

The doctor nodded. "It can be arranged."

The body was strapped into the wire basket and taken away. Ben had given up any hope of being home by one. Dan Means was covering the house with Catelli's people. Ben said to Spence, "For a start, how about this. She lets him in. He's looking for something."

"How about she comes back and finds him. She goes out and comes back and finds him?"

"Dressed that way?"

"Oh! Sure. Okay. She lets him in."

"He only looks in one place, in those cans. After that he kills her. Maybe she tried to get a knife out of that open drawer. The flour under her means he killed her after he looked. It was on his clothes and his shoes. It came off while he was banging her against the sink."

They found Catelli in the bedroom taking prints. It was a requirement Catelli despised. In his fifteen years of lab work he had yet to lift a print that had anything to do with the solution of a crime.

"You get to Bronson?" Ben asked.

"Yeah. Trenchio vacuumed his clothes and his shoes We got him another pair out of his closet and took his."

Ben turned to Dan Means. "You stay on here and see what you can dig up. Al and I'll take Bronson down. Seal it when you're through."

Lee Bronson was put in a small interview room on the second floor and left there. Wixler had made certain long ago that it was a very barren room. A bare room. No view from the window. Nothing on the walls. The only objects in the room were a small gilt radiator under the single window, a square oak table, three chairs and an ash tray made from a peanut can.

Wixler left Lee Bronson alone in that room for fifty minutes. At the end of that time he had the verification from Dr. Haughton, and he knew a great deal more about Lee Bronson. He knew his brother's record, and he knew Lee's record of a single arrest and dismissal. Five minutes before he went in to talk to Bronson, Dan Means came back with an envelope he had taken from the locked drawer of the living room desk. Catelli had gone over it for prints. Wixler was puzzled by the twenty fifty-dollar bills. It did not fit the picture of Bronson. He put the envelope in his pocket.

When he went in abruptly, Lee Bronson jumped.

"Didn't mean to startle you, Mr. Bronson," he said

115

politely. He shut the door, sat down opposite Bronson, lighted a cigarette.

"I can't seem to believe it happened," Bronson said. "I saw her, but I can't believe it. I've got to let her folks know. My God, I hate to make that call."

"Do you have any idea about who did it?"

When Bronson made no immediate answer, Wixler felt the old and familiar flicker of excitement deep inside him, an excitement that did not change the expression on his face. He had good success, a good record, with his method of interrogation. No notes, no threats, no bullying. Just quiet conversation, politeness, the kind of reassurance that kept the other man's guard down.

"Did you talk to Dr. Haughton?"

"I didn't. But we got a statement from him. He verified the time you spent with him. He kept trying to act as a character witness."

"I'd like to have you talk to him. I want him to tell you what I told him tonight. I went to him for advice. He told me to go to the police. I was going to come here tomorrow. I had decided to do that. It will . . . sound better if you get it from him."

Wixler looked at the smoke rising from his cigarette. "Is it about Danny?"

Bronson stared at him. "Yes! But how . . ."

"Pretend I'm Dr. Haughton, Lee. Forget what happened tonight. Tell me just what you told him. Tell me in the same way you told him."

Bronson told the story of Keefler, of sensing that Lucille had lied, of the money she said Danny had left with her on September twenty-eighth. He told of Keefler's threats and his own vulnerable position. Under questioning he told the complete story of his single arrest, the story that did not appear in the records. He also told of his relationship with Nick Bouchard, and his relationship with Danny, and the help they both had given him.

At that moment Al Spence, in accordance with standard procedure, opened the door and asked Ben if he'd like coffee. If Ben was not receiving co-operation he would say, "A little later." If he was, he would say yes. Al brought in the battered steaming pot, the heavy white mugs, sugar, and milk.

Wixler said in a tone that made Al glance at him in surprise, "I want Johnny Keefler. Get him and bring him in and hold him for me. Don't tell him a damn thing. When I talk to him, I want him to be sweaty."

When Al closed the door Wixler took the envelope out of his pocket and tossed it on the table. "Danny left this?"

Bronson examined it and gave Wixler a rueful look. "Good thing I brought it up, eh?"

"It helped. We're both thinking of something, Lee. For you, it's a hell of a thing to have to think about. But we better get it out in the open. Since the world began, a lot of people have been in the same spot. Your wife is dead, and you know who we're thinking about."

"Danny," Lee said in a small voice. He knotted his fist and hit it very lightly against the edge of the table, three times. His face was contorted, a white patch around his mouth.

"Let's kick it around a little. He came to see her over two weeks ago when you were out and left the money. You took it. So he came tonight to get it back and lost his head when he couldn't find it and killed her. Go for that?"

Lee shook his head slowly. "No. Danny isn't that . . . violent. If he came after it, she'd tell him I had it. And she'd have a pretty good idea it was in that locked drawer of my desk. If he had to have it, he'd have broken the lock and taken it."

"A wanted man can lose his nerve and his head."

"Danny's been wanted before."

"But not for that long a time. And if he could be clipped for something else when he was picked up, it would be the fourth fall, the big one. Life as an habitual."

"I still can't see it that way, Sergeant. I can't see him killing Seel. I know that you can think I'm being senti-mental because he's my brother, but I can't see it. And I don't know why he'd be opening those canisters and dumping the stuff out. That wasn't where she hid the money. She hid it in a brown shoulder bag on a back hook in her closet."

"Maybe something else was hidden in your house. Try that for size. She lied to you once about what he left. Maybe he left more money, a big amount."

Wixler watched Bronson's face, saw the faraway look of deep thought, saw the look of speculation and conviction. "She acted strange lately. It could be that. Danny is into something. He could be tied in with somebody. And they came after the money. If Danny knew where it was hidden, he wouldn't have opened all three canisters, would he?"

"Unless there was something hidden in each."

"Oh! I didn't think of that. But if he hid it and then came after it, wouldn't Seel have given it to him? She was hiding it for him."

"What if it was too much money, and what if your wife decided to risk taking it and making a run for it? Pardon me, but I've gathered this wasn't the happiest marriage in the world."

"It wasn't." Bronson frowned. "You know, she was very . . . considerate today. She made a big production out of lunch. That wasn't like her."

"As if she was fixing the last lunch she'd fix for you?"

"It . . . it could have been that way."

"And suppose Danny arrived at the wrong moment, as she was getting ready to take off?"

"Even so, Sergeant, he could have made her tell where she moved it to. He . . . he's an expert. Nick and Kennedy used him for that kind of thing. He wouldn't have to kill her."

"Unless she could do some talking that would hurt him."

"Then he wouldn't have done it that way. It wouldn't have been . . . so messy. He's a professional."

Wixler had the tired feeling that Bronson was probably right. The murder had that distinctive look of amateur passion and violence. It would be pleasantly easy to convince yourself Danny Bronson had done it. He wondered how far along Catelli was. He might be able to add something.

"Have some more coffee, Lee. I'll be back in a few minutes."

Catelli had nearly finished. The prints had just come from the dark room, and he was labeling them. He reported to Ben in his usual disorganized way.

"The guy got blood on his shoe, the left shoe, on the outside near the toe. Right about here. Two steps in the kitchen and then we don't get the next couple, and then we get one on the bottom step of the back porch. The ground was soft but the son of a bitch stayed on that little walk, so we lost him there. Now these here are off the big can, the one that had the flour in it. These are hers. Two good ones and a fair one."

"Recent?"

"From the oil, today or yesterday. Now we got this. An old one. Half the tip of the middle finger—not enough to give the I.D. Dan Means tells me to check with prints on file from a Daniel Bronson. It matches perfect."

"As fresh as hers?"

"No. Nowhere near. If I got to guess, I'd say over a week old. Pretty well dried out."

"Will it stand up? Is there enough?"

"Stand up! Check it yourself, Sarge. Look at this here whorl, and see this scar right through it like a kinda thin cut? Anyhow, I got a better one even."

"Where?"

"Dan Means tells me that figuring the way she was stacked I should give the bedroom the real business. You see that little table between the beds? It's got a glass top on it. I wisht all the tables in the world got glass tops. The glass is lousy with her prints and her husband's. But look at these here? First and second fingers of the right hand. Strangers! Here's the picture of the table where I circled the place we lifted them. Daniel Bronson, clear as a damn bell. Honest to God, if these nail him, I'm going to start believing in this crap."

Wixler looked at the picture of the table. A man would have to be in her bed or sitting on the edge of her bed to leave his prints in that position on the table.

"How old, Catelli?"

"Not as old as the ones on the flour can, Sarge. Not that old. But not real fresh. Don't pin me down. I'll put it this way. If her prints on the can are today, and his print on the can is a week old, then this comes somewhere in the middle. Three days, five days. Hell, I can't tell for sure."

"But you would swear they weren't made on the same day."

Catelli looked at him with an expression of outrage. "I *know* they weren't made on the same day. The oil was . . ."

"Okay, okay. How about the money Dan found?"

"Nothing. You expect anything?"

"Not really. Knobs and latches?"

"Still nothing. Not even any kind of little piece of a print on the inside knob of the back door. It turns hard, so it looks like he had gloves or else he wiped it."

Ben went back up to the room where Bronson waited. Bronson looked at him with an odd expression.

"What's the matter?"

"I just remembered the last thing I ever said to her. I leaned down and yelled in her face. I yelled 'Shut up,' and then I left."

That memory made up Wixler's mind for him. It would hurt Lee, but hurt him in a different way than he was punishing himself. In a dispassionate voice he told him what Catelli had found—the evidence of at least two visits, and the indicative place where the more recent prints were found.

"From three to five days ago?" Bronson said blankly. "In the bedroom?"

He stood up quickly and went to the window and looked out at the brick wall eight feet away, his back to the room. Wixler waited. Bronson stood there for at least two full minutes. Then he turned slowly and came back and sat down. "That *is* something Danny would do. But not without an invitation. And I don't think he just happened to sit on the bed and watch her hide the money. Not Danny. I wonder just how many other God damn invitations she passed around, and how many acceptances she had."

"Take it easy."

"I feel like a fool. That's something about her I should have been able to guess. When you get Danny I want to see him."

"I may want to talk to you again tomorrow."

"You're not holding me?"

"I don't see why we should. But I'll tell you one thing. If you wore a size twelve and a half shoe instead of an eleven, we might have solved your housing problem. I'd rather you didn't stay at home. I don't imagine you want to, do you?"

"No."

"I'll have Detective Spence take you back there while you pick up what you'll need. When you find a place to stay, phone in and let me know. By the way, Dr. Haughton is getting someone to take your classes. This is going to be a big thing in the newspapers."

They walked downstairs together. Lee Bronson stuck out his hand. Wixler hesitated, and then took it. He said, "I think we'll crack this as soon as we can get hold of your brother."

"Thanks for being . . . so damn decent, Sergeant."

Wixler watched him join Al Spence at the door and go out. He met Dan Means outside the door of the ready room.

"Got Keefler?"

"Fifteen minutes ago, Ben."

"Sit in on this with me."

"I never liked that guy, believe me."

"You aren't alone. Let's take him upstairs. You bring him."

Keefler came in with an air of arrogance. "I don't know what you fellas think you're doing, Wixler. I'm working and I get hauled in off the street like a bum or something."

"Where was he?"

"Plato's bar on Fifth Street."

"I was looking for a guy," Keefler said.

"Sit down and lower your voice, Keefler," Wixler said. Keefler hesitated and then sat down, expression defiant. "Now I am going to point out a few things to you. You are no longer a member of the force."

"Don't you think I . . ."

"Shut up."

"I got a license for a gun and your stooges took it off . . ."

"I told you to shut up. If you don't, I swear to God you spend the night in the tank and I talk to you in the morning."

Keefler looked at Wixler and then at Dan Means. He wiped his mouth on the back of his hand. "Okay, what am I supposed to have done?"

"You reported Danny Bronson as being in violation of parole."

"Right."

"Your responsibility ended there."

"Not if I can find him, it don't."

"It ended there. If your case load isn't heavy enough, ask for more. Bronson is a police responsibility."

"Okay, so I look for him anyway. Show me a law. Show me why I can't."

"You threatened a private citizen. Mr. Lee Bronson."

"He's another punk like his lousy brother."

Ben looked over at Dan Means. "I think I will put in an official complaint, Dan. I think this little viper ought to be in some new kind of work."

"He's a hero, remember," Dan said. "He shot an unarmed fourteen-year-old kid between the eyes after the kid blew his hand off."

"I don't believe Mr. Keefler should be permitted to carry a gun, and I don't believe he should be permitted to attempt to intimidate private citizens. I think we'll fix his hash in the morning."

Keefler began to yell. Spittle sprayed the table top. He slapped the table top with his good hand. For a time he was entirely incoherent. Wixler watched him mildly and then with more interest as Keefler became understandable. ". . . know a frigging thing about police work! So where is Danny? He'll be in when I bring him in. I got leads. What do you jokers know? I know he's on a blackmail kick and he's working solo or maybe with a woman and when I got pulled in I was on the track of a statement in an envelope he's got planted with somebody for insurance."

"Hold it!" Ben snapped.

"Sure. Now you listen. Now you sit up. Sure."

"What envelope? How did you hear about an envelope?"

"I'm not a cop so it's my private business."

"Lock him up, Dan."

"On what charge? What's going on?"

"Suppressing evidence. It seems a crime was committed, Johnny. Somebody killed Lucille Bronson. They were looking for something in the Bronson house. So talk. Or get booked as a common criminal."

"The envelope. You want to know about that. Okay, he was in town Thursday, Bronson was. Last Thursday, and no smart cop made him and picked him up. He went to a lawyer. He tried to get the lawyer—his name is Paul Verney—to hold a statement for him. Verney didn't like the way he acted. So he checked later, after he turned him down, and yesterday he got hold of me, and Verney give me some leads, some first names, Fred and Tommy, guys Bronson said would hold it for him. I checked the first names through CR and I been checking the list. So all the time Bronson had it! I seen them Saturday. They lied to me. You got him in a cell? I want to talk to that guy."

"Sit down. You're not talking to anybody."

Keefler sat down sullenly.

"Why did Verney contact you?"

"He found out I was Bronson's parole officer."

"Were you going to go see the Lee Bronsons again?"

"If the lead didn't check out. I was going to rough 'em a little and see if they knew about any papers Danny could have left. Now that you guys know I've been doing some good, you can stop kidding me about getting me fired off this parole thing. I can do good in that job and I like it. How about letting me help on the killing?"

Ben Wixler looked at the long, loose-mouthed face with its stain of viciousness. He let the silence grow. Keefler, during his police career, had typified the kind of officer Wixler despised.

"Johnny, I wouldn't let you put an overtime tag on a tricycle. I don't think you should be permitted to be in legal contact with any paroled convict. I think it was a sad mistake to give you the job. And I'm going to make it my business to see that it's taken away from you. Your

123

police pension will carry you. And if you are found meddling in police affairs in any way from now on, I can assure you that you will handled with the utmost severity. Don't try to bring up your record because I know your record, and it stinks. And don't hint about any influential friends, because I don't think you have a friend in the city. Now you can go."

Keefler did not move for perhaps ten seconds. Then he made his previous tirade sound, by comparison, mild and reasonable. Wixler watched the contortions, listened to the invective, and suddenly realized without great surprise, the man was insane. He glanced at Dan and Dan moved closer to Keefler. Keefler's scene was shocking, disturbing. Wixler found himself following a tiny thread of coherence. There was something about somebody named Mose being knifed to death. And some names, and deaths told of with smacking satisfaction. Rillyer. Gennetti. Casey.

"... soft!" Keefler yelled. "Every damn one of you! Mush! Soup! You gotta go after the bastards. You got to get 'em one way or another. Get 'em off the streets. Any way you can. Got to get 'em like I got Kowalsik. Filth! They're all filth! They killed Mose. They tried to kill me. You mushbellies don't understand what it is to be a cop. You don't . . ."

Ben Wixler let the words fade from his consciousness as he leafed through old files, old names. The open file on murder was much larger in Hancock than it should have been. He had been through the file many times. Many of the murders had been committed long before he had joined the force, but there was no statute of limitations on murder. He remembered the grimy label on the faded file folder, a folder of a type no longer in use. Kowalsik, Gilbert Peter. And a particularly unsavory glossy photograph of the body flashed into his mind. Tortured to death. Body found in the lake.

"... try to lose me my job, a pansy cop like you, and I'll go to every paper in town and I'll . . ."

"Shut your mouth!" Ben roared. It startled Dan Means as much as it startled Keefler. Keefler sagged back in the chair.

"I want to hear just a little bit more about how you

124

got Gilbert Kowalsik, Johnny," he said gently. "Tell me a little bit more."

Keefler looked at Wixler. He snapped his head around and looked at Dan Means. His eyes were wide and staring and curiously blank. He looked like a man suddenly awakening from a sound sleep. His eyes narrowed. He looked down at his artificial hand. In far too casual a voice he said, "I didn't say anything about Gil Kowalsik. I don't know where you got an idea like that."

Ben didn't even have to glance at Dan Means to have him come in on cue. "We both heard you, Johnny. We want to know about it."

"Tell us," Ben said. "First you called him just Kowalsik. I called him Gilbert Kowalsik, but you called him Gil. I guess you know him pretty well."

"Gil? Oh! Oh, sure, I knew Gil. When I was a kid. I think he got killed. I remember something about it. A long time ago, I think."

"But, Johnny. You didn't say you fixed him. You didn't use a word like that. You said you 'got' him. I think you were explaining how a *good* cop takes the law into his own hands. We both heard you, Johnny. We just want to know how you got Kowalsik."

"You guys are nuts. I didn't say anything about him. You didn't hear me right."

Ben leaned back. "You know something? We got all night, Johnny. All night long. Dan, suppose you go pull the Kowalsik file. Check the estimated time of death. Send somebody into dead records to pull Keefler's duty reports for the estimated time of death. Bring the file back up here. And bring a fresh pot of coffee."

"You guys are way off the beam," Keefler mumbled.

"We've got all the time in the world, Johnny."

The sedan pulled away and Ben walked up his front walk in the first pale gray of dawn. He managed to undress so quietly Beth didn't stir. But when he eased himself into bed the sag of the bed aroused her.

"'Lo, honey," she murmured. "Gosh, s'nearly morning."

"Go to sleep, baby."

125

She braced herself on one elbow and looked at him. "You got the grumps, haven't you? Bad night?"

"I've got to be back at nine. We've got a hot one. But I guess it was a good night. We took an old one off the books. Got a confession. In detail. Seems a cop did it."

"Oh, honey! How awful for you!"

"An ex-cop, but he was a cop when he did it, and I personally think he's been crazy all his life, and he did it in a way that turned my stomach and I . . . The hell with it. Good night, baby."

She kissed him. "Sleep fast because you haven't got much sleeping time, darling."

CHAPTER TEN

Paul Verney

Verney awoke at six on Wednesday morning. During the first few moments of consciousness he wondered only why the alarm had been set so early, and then it all came roaring back into his mind. He remembered the curious things that had happened to him after he had grabbed the woman. It seemed that he had stood a little bit aside from himself and heard the hollow metallic sound as he kept slamming her head against the edge of the sink. It seemed to him that he had gotten back into himself with an effort. She had seemed utterly without weight. Only as he had regained control had he felt the slack heaviness of her and realized she was dead and had been dead for many long seconds.

He had let her slip from his hands and thud to the floor, and he had backed away from her. He remembered telling himself to look at the scene coldly and objectively and see if he had left any clue. Yet in the very next second, it seemed, he was walking down a dark street, walking too fast, breathing too hard, with absolutely no memory of having left the house. He had slowed and stopped, thinking that he should go back and empty drawers and make it look as though a thief had been in the house. Maybe he should take some small things of value and dispose of them.

And again, frighteningly without transition, he found himself trying to turn the door handle of his locked car three blocks from the Bronson house. As he hunted in his pockets for the car keys, he saw the telltale white on the front of his topcoat and on his shoes. He stamped his shoes hard, frantically dusted the white flour from the front of his topcoat. He was still breathing very fast, very deeply, as though he had been running.

He got into the car and he started to think of how the fragile nape of the neck had felt in his right hand . . . and he was putting his key into the door of his room on the third floor of the Center Club. The hiatus frightened him. It was as though his brain kept cutting out, as though a wire to some essential terminal came loose.

Once he was in his locked room, and deep in the leather chair, his mind began to function in the orderly way he depended upon.

No one had seen him go to her house. No one, he hoped, had seen him leave it. Because it was a self-service elevator, and there was no attendant on the front desk of the club after six, no one could prove how long he had been away from the club. As there was no note under his door, there had been no phone call and no visitor during the hour and a half he had been gone. He was certain no one had seen him in the heavy shadows where he had stood and watched them eat, and watched the man drive away.

The girl had been vapid and easily handled. He inspected his clothing and his shoes and found them clean of flour. He took the statement Bronson had written from his topcoat pocket, read it through again. It would have been infinitely damaging. He held it until the flame scorched his fingers, and dropped it into the toilet and flushed it. The girl had known about the money. Her death had been essential. Yet it would have been essential anyway, once he had the statement. Because the statement was a warrant for Bronson's death. He wondered if he would have had the nerve to wait for the man and kill him also if she had not revealed that the man was ignorant of the statement Bronson had left.

The next step was to meet with Danny Bronson before he could get word of the death of his sister-in-law. It would have to be early. Before Bronson was up, and listening to a news broadcast. It was likely that he slept late. It could all go wrong if Danny Bronson was not at the camp. But again it was unlikely he would leave and take a chance of getting picked up on the morning of the day he expected to receive the money.

Before going to bed he prepared three articles—a suitcase with enough books in it to give it a convincing weight, a note to leave at the front desk downstairs asking Harry to please call his office at nine and tell them he would be in a little later than usual, and a Belgian .32 automatic with a full clip. He had taken it from a hot-tempered client many years before, and knew it was untraceable.

He dressed hurriedly. He left the note on the front desk, carried the suitcase through the club to his car parked in the rear. It was a clear morning, a chill morning, smelling of the coming of winter. The automatic was in the right hand pocket of his top coat. As he drove he rehearsed exactly how he would do it, and where he would do it, and how it would be.

He turned down the gravel road, rounded the curve by the woods and saw the camp ahead, the gray sedan parked behind it. He pulled in beside the sedan, raced his motor, then gave a prolonged blast on his car horn. He got out and put the suitcase on the ground beside him and waited. He gave another blast, picked up the suitcase and walked around the camp to the terrace. He laid the suitcase flat on the metal-topped table, stood slightly beyond the table, his hands in his topcoat pocket. He wormed his right hand into the black leather glove and found the trigger guard with his first finger.

Danny Bronson came out of the door, hair tousled, face thick and ugly with sleep. He wore a pale blue terrycloth robe.

"What the hell, Verney?"

"I brought it."

"Hell it's not eight o'clock yet."

"Shall I take it away and bring it back this afternoon? Would that suit you better? Frankly, I don't like driving around with that much money in the car."

Bronson moved closer and touched the suitcase with his fingertips. "Where's the good five grand?"

"Inside. It's separately wrapped."

Danny thumbed back the latches to raise the top. When both his hands were in sight, thumbs on the two brass latches, Paul Verney yanked the automatic out of his pocket and, from a distance of four feet, with arm outstretched, he shot Bronson full in the face. The shot made a feeble snapping sound in the open air. Bronson yelled harshly and staggered back, arms lifting. Verney fired at the broad chest. He felt coldly competent. He aimed at the left side of the chest. Bronson fell awkwardly. Verney stepped around the table. Bronson was looking up, face agonized, mouth working. Verney put the gun six inches from Bronson's broad forehead and fired again.

... and then he was bending over Bronson who lay quite dead on his back and he had the muzzle against the dead forehead and he was pulling the trigger and it was not working and his finger ached from pulling it so hard, and he did not know how long he had been there.

He straightened up. There was a hole beside Bronson's nose. There was a stain no larger than a quarter on the left side of the chest of the blue robe. There were five holes in the tan forehead, and all could have been covered by a silver dollar.

... and he was driving down the gravel road and swerved violently when the big convertible swung around the corner, and he put his right wheels in the shallow ditch. The car stopped opposite him and Drusilla Catton rolled down her window, leaned toward him and said with consternation, "What in the world are you doing here, Paul?"

"Dru," he said quickly, "Dru, I'm so glad to see you. There's something I must talk to you about. I . . . I'll ride down to the camp with you."

"But . . ."

"I've talked to Bronson. He . . . he was going to tell you but I can tell you."

He got in beside her. "Goodness!" she said. "I've never seen you so upset. You're actually dithering like a girl. Old solemn rock Verney. I guess you know about Danny and me."

"Yes."

"And maybe you want to give me a fatherly talk. I

130

hope to hell not, Paul. I happen to know exactly what I'm doing."

"I suppose you know Danny is trying to blackmail me?"

She giggled. "I rather imagined he'd try that the moment he forced it out of me. Yes, I knew he was. Does it make you squirm, Paul dear?"

She parked behind the house. He knew she would see Danny the moment she walked around the house. A coherent and reasonable plan was beginning to form in his mind. It had looked lost for a time, but this could be even better. This could result in a better kind of deception.

He got out of the car as she did, and put the heavy leather gloves on quickly. As she started around the side of the house, he came up behind her. He took a single deep breath and locked his forearm across her throat. Her body spasmed with astonishing strength. He was swung off balance and he fell heavily, without losing his hold on her. When she tried to reach back for his face, he turned his face down behind her shoulder, his cheek against her back. Her struggle rolled them completely over. A sharp heel dug into his shin. He held her tightly. He felt her body begin to loosen. Her shoe scraped on the walk.

. . . and he lay holding her, his arm cramped, his eyes squeezed tightly shut, and he had no way of knowing how long he had been there. It was difficult for him to unbend his locked arm. He got up and staggered weakly and caught his balance. As he left her, the body sagged onto its back. The bloated face was frightful, and he looked away from it. He listened to the sounds of the morning. A commercial airliner went over, already settling for the landing at Hancock. He suppressed the desire to run. They could see nothing from such a height.

He stood for a long time, planning just what he would do. He carried her into the house, dangling over his shoulder, arms around her slack legs. He sat her carefully on the edge of the bed, the huge bed, and let her fall back. It took him a long time to undress her. His hands in the leather gloves were clumsy, and the job was distasteful, and much more difficult than he had imagined it would be. He was going to put her into the bed and then, remembering the violence of her struggle, he pushed her off onto the floor on the other side of the bed. Her head struck the hardwood floor with an impact that made his stomach twist.

He put her clothing away carefully.

In a small shed apart from the house he found what he needed. A length of heavy insulated wire, some cinder blocks. He carried wire and cinder blocks down to the dock and lowered them into the green rowboat tied up there. He got Danny under the arms and dragged him down, tumbled the body into the boat. He wired the cinder blocks firmly to Danny's ankles, rowed out into the middle of the artificial lake. The water was glassy calm. The boat made a long wake. He lifted legs and blocks over the side. He pushed Danny into a sitting position on the side of the boat. The boat tipped and suddenly he was gone. Cold water was splashed into Verney's face. The boat rocked violently, shipping some water. When it was still again he looked down. He could not see him. He rowed back and tied up the boat.

He went back into the house and looked for the keys to the gray sedan. He looked everywhere. He found them just as he was beginning to become frantic. They were in an ash tray on a table near the living room door. He took a last look around, and was glad he did. He hooked up a hose from the shed to an outside faucet and rinsed off the flagstones where Danny's head had been, rinsed off the blood and flecks of tissue and a single curved fragment of bone.

He drove the sedan up the gravel road, watching the ditch carefully. When he saw a deep enough place, he backed up, then ran the car violently into the ditch. It shook him up badly, and he bit the inside of his lower lip. He raced the motor in gear until the back wheels were buried deep. He left the keys in it, got into his own car, rocked it until it came up out of the shallow ditch.

Verney was in his office by eleven o'clock. He told his secretary he had driven out toward Kemp to look at some property that might come on the market soon. She gave him the phone messages and said a policeman named

132

Spence had stopped in to see him at ten o'clock and said he'd be back later.

"Did he say what it was about?"

"No, sir."

The man came back at quarter to twelve and introduced himself as Detective Spence of the Homicide Section. He was a spare man with scurfy hair and a long face so dry as to look dusty. Verney was relieved by his casual manner. Spence was pleased to accept a cigar.

"I want to ask some questions about a parole officer named Keefler who came to see you the other day about a visit you got from Danny Bronson."

"Oh yes, of course."

Verney told the story of Bronson's visit, of his curiosity about the man and about the suspicious way he had acted. And he related his conversation with Keefler.

"We got Keefler locked up for murder."

"Keefler! Indeed?"

"An oldie from way back. He got excited and spilled it to Sergeant Ben Wixler. We were talking to Keefler actually about the murder of Bronson's sister-in-law last night."

"Murder?"

"How could you miss it, Mr. Verney?"

"I'm afraid I did. I haven't seen a paper yet and I haven't heard the radio newscasts."

Spence stood up. "It was about this same thing, we think. About the envelope, the same one he tried to leave with you. Wixler will get to the bottom of it. He nearly always does. Danny is about nineteen times as hot as he was yesterday."

"This Sergeant Wexler thinks Bronson did it?"

"Not Wexler. Wixler. I don't know exactly what he thinks, Mr. Verney. I know he wants to talk to Danny."

"If you ever find out what was in that envelope, I would like very much to know, Mr. Spence."

"We'll find out. We always do. See you around," Spence said, and drifted out.

Verney tried to compose himself after Spence had gone. There had been something peculiarly disquieting about the man. He had the air of utter casual confidence.

We always do.

He quieted himself with logical thought. Four people had known or could make a good guess at the contents of that envelope. Mrs. Lee Bronson, Drusilla Catton, Danny Bronson and himself. And he was certainly never going to share that knowledge with anybody.

In review he decided that he had moved quickly and deftly, and had improvised well. He had done something distasteful to him and yet necessary to his well-being. Three had died. A pretty, superficial, shallow young woman. A trashy older woman. A wanted man. There was no loss to society.

It would be well, he decided, to set up the date of his trip to South America.

CHAPTER ELEVEN

Ben Wixler

Inspector Wendell Matthews sat at his ease in Ben Wixler's office, chair tilted back, chubby knee sharply bent, right heel caught on the edge of the chair, hands laced around his right ankle. It was ten o'clock on the morning of Thursday, October eighteenth.

Matthews was a round man who, twenty years before, had barely met minimum height requirements. He had thinning brown hair, ice gray eyes and a small petulant mouth. He had the reputation of being a fusspot, an old lady who looked for dust in the corners and under the rugs, who looked for incorrect entries in the files, who was death on coffee breaks. The few in the department who knew him better knew that only the surface of his mind was occupied with departmental trivia. Ben Wixler and a handful of others had a good deal of respect for the quiet logic underneath.

They had been discussing the available facts in the Bronson murder, and Matthews had gone over the already bulky file.

"This could hurt you," Matthews said.

"What am I doing that I shouldn't do? What haven't I done that should be done, Wendy? We've gone through that neighborhood thoroughly. Danny Bronson is as hot as anybody can be. It looks like we have to wait until he's found."

"You know what I mean, Ben. You read the papers. Professor's wife slain. Huge manhunt for paroled convict. Mystery money figures in Bronson case. She was a sexy looking item, and she loved having her picture taken. So all the wire services have picked it up. The deal of getting killed with the kitchen sink gives it that nice flavor of the macabre. Bucky Angelis, our fighting district attorney, wants in on the act."

"I know. He was over. Offering all the manpower of his office and the Special Detail, or something. But what could I use them for?"

"Bad psychology, Ben. You should have accepted, and given them a make-work job."

"Why?"

"Suppose Danny isn't located? Then you're up the creek. And it would be nice to be able to share the blame. Keep it to yourself, and you don't have too much time left."

"Before what?"

"Are you trying to needle me, Sergeant? You know damn well what I mean. Bucky will lean on the Commissioner of Public Safety. He sees a chance to get his picture in the paper. So he leans on the Police Commissioner, who leans on the Chief, who then has to fix this curious situation of having a sergeant in charge of the Homicide Section. And I will bet you a bun that fifteen minutes after you are relieved as acting head of section, Danny is picked up and the new guy unravels the deal like a home-made sweater. So then you wait another year or two because the Chief can't safely sign a promotion for some-body he has relieved of duty, no matter what he thinks privately. If you haven't gained any ground you are cer-tain to be all washed up by Monday, and it could happen as soon as tomorrow."

"You're full of cheer, Wendy."

Matthews thumped his chair down onto all four legs. "Let me check your thinking with mine on this thing. Do you think Danny Bronson killed her?"

"I'll bet about ten to one against it. I think he got into bed with her, and I think he was using her as a drop for money and maybe something else important to him—a statement protecting him from somebody he was gouging. I've done some research on Danny Bronson. He is tough, greedy, and brutal. He's also intelligent and remarkably unlucky. What he is doesn't fit the crime."

136

"Lee Bronson?"

"Not a chance. There is a nice guy."

"That's why you count him out?"

"Now who's needling who? We've triple-checked the time he arrived at Haughton's against the earliest possible time of death. If he could cross the city in ten seconds, he could have done it."

"So who do you nominate?"

"Either Mr. X or Mr. Y. Mr. X is an associate of Danny's. I have a choice of motives for Mr. X. Either Danny got a big payoff and hid it at the Bronson house and Mr. X went there and got it—or Mr. X wanted to get hold of Danny's insurance statement and find out what Danny had on the blackmailee, who we will call Mr. Y. There is only one motive for Mr. Y. To get out from under Danny. To do that he had to find where the statement was hidden and go get it, and he had to also eliminate Danny, either before or after getting the statement. I would vote for the elimination of Danny taking place after he got his hands on the statement. It would be safer that way."

"Who do you like best?"

"My man is Mr. Y. He didn't leave any clues, and he was very clever about being unobserved, but the actual killing itself had . . . an amateur flavor. It was a murder of convenience, and yet it was brutal and uncontrolled enough to look like a murder of passion."

Matthews knuckled his small round chin. "So you think our Danny may be dead too?"

"If my logic is acceptable, I think there's a good chance of it."

"Then you're really in the bag."

"If the body had been hidden carefully enough."

"Your Mr. Y would be a substantial citizen."

"Important, anyway. And rich enough to make it worth Danny's efforts. And desperate enough to take a hell of a chance. We don't know much about him. We know he's a big man, powerful. We know he's got something to hide. We can guess that somehow Danny came in contact with him and found out what he's hiding. We've had no luck trying to backtrack on Danny. He's avoided all usual

137

haunts and acquaintances, at least since the end of June."

"The big flaw is how he'd get a tough monkey like Danny Bronson to tell him where the statement . . ."

Matthews stopped as the phone rang and Ben picked it up. Ben pulled a pad toward him and began scribbling on it. "Yes. Sure, I remember you, Captain. Route 90. Turn off three miles this side of Kemp. I see what you mean. Yes. Well, I won't waste any time. An hour."

Ben hung up. He grinned broadly at Matthews. "Want to go for a little ride?"

"What's up?"

"That was Captain Donovan of the CI Bureau of the State Police. He's found out where Danny has been living."

Ben Wixler, Al Spence, and Inspector Matthews went out to the Catton camp. As it was outside their jurisdiction, and as they were present on invitation, it would have been impertinent to arrive with lab people or with too many people. Donovan had invited them in because of the connection with the Bronson murder.

With Ben directing the driver, they found the gravel road and turned in. A gray sedan was mired in a deep ditch just beyond where the road curved around the edge of a wood. They were then in sight of the camp.

"Nice layout," Spence said. "Complete with four trooper cars."

"The convertible there has Hancock plates," Matthews noted.

Captain Donovan came to meet them as they got out of the car. He was an enormous brown man with a resolute stride, military bearing, puffy eyes and a parade-ground voice. He knew both Wixler and Matthews and was introduced to Spence, who winced visibly at the Captain's handshake.

"I'll give you the history to date," Donovan roared. "The Kemp Barracks got a routine call last night about midnight, somebody who wouldn't give their name saying there was a car stuck in the ditch, that one you saw as you drove in. It was a young voice and it's a good guess some neckers drove in and saw it and couldn't find

138

anybody around and reported it. Trooper Jensen out of Kemp checked it at about twelve-thirty and got the license number and drove in here to the house and couldn't raise anybody, even though that convertible was parked right where it is now. The whole thing looked a little funny to him, so instead of waiting until morning, we got a night check on the licenses, something we've been fighting for for ten years and didn't get until this year. The convertible sedan is registered to a Mr. Jack Young in Kemp, but it turns out the address is a phony. At three this morning Jensen was directed to come back here and check the house, and another trooper was assigned with him.

"When they knocked and received no answer, they entered the house and in the bedroom they found the body of a woman approximately thirty years of age, dark hair. She was nude and had been strangled to death. They radioed Kemp Barracks and immediate contact was made with my office and with the Sheriff's office. I contacted the Sheriff, received his verbal request for assistance, and set out with specialists from my office, arriving here at five thirty-five this morning.

"After a quick inspection of the premises, I telephoned Mr. Burton Catton in your city, but the phone was not answered. By that time a detailed investigation of the premises was under way. After examination by the county coroner, and after fingerprinting and nail-scraping, the body was removed to a funeral home in Kemp pending formal identification and autopsy if deemed necessary by the county coroner. My fingerprint people, in going over this house, have acquired two complete sets of prints. One of them matches the prints of the woman. The other set was broken down into numerical analysis, for transmittal to central records in the area and, if unidentified, to Washington. It was obvious from the distribution of the prints that the man and woman involved had been living in this house for an extended period."

When Donovan paused for breath, Ben noticed that Al Spence was regarding the big man with a look of awe bordering on consternation. Donovan could have been heard clearly at two hundred feet.

"Having had your advice that one Daniel Bronson,

139

wanted for suspicion of murder, has been hiding out in the general area of Hancock, and seeing how excellent a place this would be, I directed that the numerical analysis be checked by radio against the analysis on record for Bronson's prints. When I discovered that the second set of prints belong to Daniel Bronson, I telephoned you as a matter of courtesy and co-operation. Subsequent to phoning you, I tried the telephone for Mr. Burton Catton for the fourth time, and the phone was answered by Mr. Catton. When I said that I had phoned him earlier, he explained that due to illness he had had a night switch placed on his phone so as not to be disturbed during the night. I asked him if his wife was at home. He excused himself from the phone, returned in approximately one minute and said that she was not in, nor had her bed been slept in. As I had identified myself, he seemed upset. I asked him to describe his wife. In size, age and coloring, his description matched the body. I asked him if he knew a Mr. Johnson, and described the location of this house. Mr. Catton explained that this was his house, that he hadn't been here in over a year. He was not aware it was being used. I requested that he come here. After I have questioned him further, he can make formal identification of the body. He has not yet arrived. There are some other details I can easier show than explain. Other than that, are there any questions?"

"How long had the woman been dead?"

"The estimate is twenty hours from the time of examination of the body. That would place it about eight o'clock yesterday morning. Now, if you gentlemen will follow me, I will show you where the body was discovered."

They followed Donovan through the camp. His voice, inside four walls, seemed much more powerful. His men were still at work in the camp. They went back out onto the terrace. Captain Donovan said, "This would seem to me to be the logical reconstruction. Bronson and the Catton woman quarreled and he strangled her. He left here in a panic, taking no time to pack. In his hurry, he drove carelessly and put his car in the ditch. He did not come back and take her car as it is far too conspicuous an automobile. My belief is that he walked out to Route 90 and hitchhiked."

One of the troopers came around the corner of the building and said, "Taxi coming, sir."

"That should be Mr. Catton. Will you join me?"

They followed Donovan around to the parking area. A Hancock taxi had stopped and a man was getting out of it. He moved feebly, with great caution. His face was a pasty color. He looked apologetically at Donovan and said, "I haven't driven since . . . my illness."

"I'll see that you get transportation for your return, Mr. Catton. You can pay him now."

The driver said, "It's going to be just the same as I told you, mister. I got to go back empty, don't I?" He took the money Catton handed him and said, "Thanks. What's going on here? A cop convention?"

"Roll it!" Donovan bellowed into the window. The cab left, the rear tires spinning gravel.

Catton, looking around, noticed Matthews for the first time. He smiled, and with the pathetic ghost of what had once been an impressive joviality, said, "Why, hello, Wendy! Wendy, maybe you'll tell me what is going on."

"This is Captain Donovan's party, Burt. He wants to ask you some questions about Dru."

"I know it's about Dru. She didn't come home at all. I don't know what . . . Could I sit down somewhere, please?"

"Surely," Donovan yelled. They went back around the building and Catton sank gratefully into one of the terrace chairs. Donovan pulled another chair so close their knees were almost touching. A uniformed man appeared and sat near by, notebook on knee.

"When is the last time you saw your wife, Mr. Catton?"

"Let me think. The day before yesterday. Tuesday. In our apartment at five o'clock. She came in and showered and changed and went out again."

"Did she say where?"

Catton tried to smile. "I'm afraid that . . . since my illness, we haven't paid much attention to each other. I haven't been as interested in her activities as . . . I once

141

was. She came and went as she pleased. She had her own friends."

"Why are you using the past tense, Mr. Catton?"

The smile was stronger, but it was an ironic smile. "I have heart trouble, not head trouble, Captain. You asked for a description. You were very heavy and mysterious. All these policemen wouldn't be around if she had . . . say, reported a theft. I must guard myself against shock, so I spent my time on the way out here getting slowly adjusted to the fact that she is probably dead. And to be thoroughly honest with you, Captain, I don't believe I care a great deal. A year ago I would have been utterly shattered. Now I can't really care. And I believe that is more selfishness than heartlessness. I am too busy being concerned about myself."

"Has she ever spoken of a man named Daniel Bronson?"

"No. Not that I recall."

"Jack Young?"

"No. Captain Donovan, can you bring yourself to tell me if she is dead? Or would that violate your code?"

"The woman found dead in this house may be your wife, Mr. Catton. We want you to look at the body."

"I'm sorry, Captain. I will not do that. I can adjust to the fact of her death, but I won't risk any possible shock from looking at her. I have had a severe coronary. A large area of the heart is damaged. I do not intend to risk the undamaged portions of it. Surely you can find someone else."

"This is very unusual."

"I can't help that. I absolutely refuse. Sorry."

"You described her in general. Is there any . . . specific or unusual marking on her body?"

"Yes. On the inside of her left thigh, just above the knee, there's a rather ugly scar. She was bitten there by a large dog when she was just old enough to walk. In those days they cauterized dog bites."

"Then I believe we can be certain it is your wife."

"I was certain it was. I didn't believe any . . . companion of my more active days would be likely to come back to the camp here. How did she die? I assume violently."

"Why do you assume that?"

"She lived violently, Captain. She was a violent woman."

"She was strangled to death."

Catton grimaced. "Very ugly death. By the way, a name you mentioned. Bronson. Isn't that the man already wanted for murder?"

"The same one."

"She was spending a great deal of time away from the apartment. Was Bronson living here?"

"We think so."

"I hope he is a man of perception and taste. A lot of time and money went into this place. Have you caught him?"

"Not yet."

"Apparently he succumbed to a temptation I used to have quite often, Captain."

"What was that?"

"To strangle Drusilla."

Donovan eyed Catton curiously, and then said, "There are expensive clothes here that would fit Bronson. Do you know if she was spending more than usual?"

"Dru was undoubtedly spending just what she has always spent, and that is all she's got. She had an income from a trust fund and I provided her with an allowance. The total seems very generous, but it was never enough for Drusilla. Never."

Though Ben Wixler was listening intently, there was something trying to force its way into his consciousness. It was a sensation he had experienced before. He knew that either he had heard something that was more significant than the surface meaning would indicate, or he had seen something slightly out of key.

He gestured to Wendy Matthews and got up and went about forty feet down toward the artifical lake. There he could hear Donovan's questions, but not Catton's answers. He saw Spence look toward him and start to get up. Ben motioned him to remain. Matthews followed Ben, obviously irritated by the interruption.

143

"What's the matter?"

"Something. I don't know. I thought I'd check with you. Have you heard anything that rang any faraway bells?"

"No. What the hell?"

"Have you seen anything odd, anything that has raised a question so faint you don't know what the question is?"

"Now I'll ask you one. Did you eat a good breakfast? Have you taken your pulse lately?"

"Okay. Sorry. Let's get back."

They went back but his attention still wandered. He began to inspect his immediate environment, almost inch by inch. The flagstones were large and irregular, and had been cemented into place. The cement between them was recessed. When his eye, traveling slowly and carefully, rested on an area to the left of the captain's chair, he felt a quiver of recognition. He saw at once what had puzzled his subconscious. In all other parts of the terrace the recessed cement strips between the flagstones were filled with pine needles, dirt and leaf scraps. In the area to the left of the captain's chair, the recessed areas were clean, and the four flagstones looked cleaner than the others. The clean strip extended toward the edge of the terrace. Had something been spilled and hosed off? Why wasn't the entire terrace hosed off? Why just one area?

He examined the four flagstones more carefully, inch by inch. The captain's right foot rested on the corner of a tan one. In the middle of the tan one he saw two small grayish marks, one larger than the other. He leaned far to one side and the grayish marks took on a faint metallic gleam.

The captain was saying, "When did you notice any change in her habits and when . . ." He broke off and stared down at Ben who was on one knee picking with his thumb nail at the larger of the two gray marks. "What in God's name are you doing, Wixler?"

"Take a look," Ben said. "Looks like this area was hosed down. And these marks are lead. Lean down and look at this little sort of gold speckle here. Copper jacket." He sat back on one heel and looked up at Donovan. "Were there any holes in the lady?"

"No!" Donovan jumped to his feet, turned toward the house. "Baker!" he bawled. A man came out of the house at almost a dead run. "Get your stuff for a blood check." Baker darted away. Donovan moved everybody to the far end of the terrace and, after a speculative glance at Wixler, continued his questioning. Baker came back and worked with his bottles and filter paper, making his way to the edge of the terrace. He came and stood by Donovan.

When Donovan looked up he held out his filter paper and said, "Positive, sir. Not enough to type, but human blood. I got the best trace where it was washed off into the grass."

"Recent?"

"I guess it would have to be. It would have to be since the last heavy rain and that was Tuesday."

"May I make a suggestion?" Ben said.

"Of course."

"Have your man check that boat down there at the dock."

Donovan stared at Ben, then his face showed comprehension and he told Baker to do so. Ben strolled down to where Baker had begun to work. Baker, kneeling in the bottom of the boat, looked up at him and grinned and said, "Jackpot. Enough to type. A big beautiful clot."

Ben looked out at the small lake, at the small chop piled up by the crisp west breeze. He turned on his heel and went back to the terrace and told Donovan what Baker was picking up.

Donovan said, "I'm sorry to have to tire you with these questions, Mr. Catton. I can have you driven back to the city immediately."

"If it's permitted, I'd like to go in the house and rest for a little while."

"It's all right now. My men are through in the house."

As Catton started toward the door, Ben said, "Excuse me, Mr. Catton. Would it be all right if we cut that dam and let the water out?"

Catton turned and looked at his lake. He said carefully, "You have my permission to blow it to hell." He continued

145

on toward the door and turned and said with a death's-head grin, "I know one thing you will find."

"What sir?"

"A great many empty bottles." He shut the door behind him.

Donovan looked at the earth dam at the end of the small lake. "Easier to blow it. I'll make arrangements." He hurried off.

Ben turned to Wendy Matthews. "Any bets?"

Matthews shook his head. "I'll take the other side, though. Fifty to one it's our Danny. And remind me never to sneer again when you get one of your strange feelings, Ben."

"I like the way the pattern is showing more clearly all the time. Danny takes up with Drusilla Catton. She is in on his scheme. It's even logical to assume she provided him with the angle to work on. But the intended victim didn't lie still and let them pick all his feathers. He got a line on where Danny had left the statement that he thought provided him with immunity. So he recovered the statement and killed Lucille Bronson and got out here early the next morning and got neatly rid of this unholy pair. There was a certain amount of cunning in hiding one body and leaving the other so we would all go running off in all directions looking for Danny. With or without that streak of luck I had, Wendy, I was going to make sure Danny's body wasn't in the lake or buried on the premises."

"So where do we go from here?"

"We find out who Drusilla Catton was chummy with during the past couple of years, so chummy she could have found out something Danny could sell back to the man."

At twelve-thirty a state trooper pushed the plunger on a small black box and four sticks of dynamite inserted deep into the earthen base of the dam made a muffled thump Ben could feel in the soles of his feet. Dirt flew high, and before it fell to earth the water of the lake had started to move out through a ragged gap in the dam. As it moved it widened the gap, and a muddy torrent galloped down the bed of the small stream. Ben watched the pilings of the dock and saw the water move slowly down, exposing the darker area of the part that had been under water. The gleaming mud flats began to appear around the shore line. As the gap widened it moved faster. In twenty minutes the lake had drained.

They stood on the shore line and watched three husky troopers, minus shoes, socks, and uniform trousers, wade out through the black mud to the body about eighty feet from shore. It lay with the head toward the break in the dam, lay face down and naked in the mud except for a soaked blue robe that covered the shoulders and the head and trailed out in the direction of the flow.

The troopers bent over the body. One worked on the ankles. Soon they headed back toward shore, two of them carrying the body by ankles and armpits, one of them carrying two cinder blocks wired together. They put the body on the dock and went up to hose the mud off their legs and dress again.

"Bronson?" Donovan asked.

"Can we get some of the mud off?" Ben asked.

A trooper brought the hose as far as it would reach. The water sprayed in a high arc and fell on the body and soon washed the face clean.

"It's Danny Bronson," Matthews said.

Donovan bent closer. "Six shots in the head. Look at these. I've never seen anything just like this before. Small stuff. Thirty-two caliber, I'd guess. Close range for these five in the forehead. Inches away." He gingerly parted the robe. "And one under the heart. Seven shots. Good guess it's an automatic."

Donovan straightened up and looked out at the black expanse of mud. "If it's out there we can get it. Two men with metal detectors could cover it in a day. They won't enjoy it, but they can do it."

Ben looked up toward the house and saw three men walking swiftly toward them. The one in the lead was Billy Sullivan, wearing a wide, wise and handsome smile. The one in the rear was slipping a plate holder into his Speed Graphic.

"Private party?" Billy asked. "Or can anybody come?"

Donovan moved forward with the ponderous inevitability of a tank and brought the three of them to a stop. "I will give you an interview containing all pertinent facts in due time, gentlemen," he roared politely at them. "If you will be so kind as to return to the parking area, I will be with you shortly."

"How shortly?" Billy asked.

"In ten minutes."

"Would that be Danny Bronson, Captain?"

"It was, at one time," he said, herding them back.

"Killed in desperate gun battle with brave officers?"

"Unfortunately no. How did you people find out about this?"

"A cab driver thought the information might be worth five bucks. After I paid him, Captain, I checked with Sergeant Wixler's office. We'll co-operate, but in all fairness this ought to be a *Ledger* exclusive."

"Ten minutes," Donovan said.

When the reporters were out of earshot, Ben said, "You aren't going to turn them loose on Catton, are you?"

"He left twenty minutes ago. Her father is going to make the formal identification." Donovan directed his men to make the necessary examination of the body and recall the county coroner. He turned back to Wixler and Matthews. "It looks like this is all tied in together, gentlemen, your little affair and mine. I have given you access to all information available to me. I suggest you inform me of your conclusions. I suspect the killer will be eventually apprehended in your city."

"Brief the Captain, Ben," Matthews said.

Ben quickly summarized his thinking, and concluded by saying, "So it's either a partner who waited until the take and then decided to keep it all himself, or it's the man they were trying to fleece. I like the second possibility. Now we can start hunting for Mr. X. We can triangulate him. Somebody who had previous contact with Danny Bronson. We know one thing. It's a big deal. It isn't a gouge for a thousand or two. And whoever they had on the hook, it wasn't information that would just maybe bust up a marriage, or get the guy thrown off the Board

148

of Education. It was something that would hurt worse. He was so vulnerable, he could rationalize some risky killing."

Donovan nodded. "Sound enough. How much, if any, of what you've said can be told to our journalistic friends?"

"Let's just let them have the facts. No guesses. Bronson's residence here, with the woman. Her death and his."

Donovan squared himself and looked challengingly at Wixler. "And why did we look in the lake?"

"In checking the area, Captain, you and your people came across evidence that there could have been a second killing."

Matthews said quietly, "Ben here hasn't all the rank he ought to have yet, Captain. There are wolves in the shrubbery."

Donovan nodded. "It won't hurt me to give away a little credit. I just wanted to know the attitude, Matthews."

"We're in the same business," Ben said.

"Sometimes Roeber forgot that." He studied Wixler. "We'll get along."

"Thanks for letting us know so quickly, Captain," Ben said. "We have to be getting back now."

As Wixler, Spence, and Matthews went to the car where the driver was still waiting, Billy Sullivan drifted over and said, "Are we going to get the brush, Ben?"

"No. He'll be fair."

"Can I come get another statement from you after I get this story in?"

"I won't be able to give you any more than he'll give you, Billy."

"You know," Billy said thoughtfully, "if I could get a rewrite man to hang out a window, he could take it direct from Donovan."

Matthews pulled the door of the sedan shut and said through the window, "The captain used to command troops."

"On windy days," Sullivan said.

They drove out and headed back toward the city. Matthews told the driver to make time. He put the sedan up to ninety, with red blinker light flashing. He touched the siren only when traffic was clotted in front of them, and the low warning growl quickly opened up a lane.

Al Spence turned around in the front seat, cigarette in the corner of his mouth bobbling as he spoke. "You act like you know where we go from here," he said.

"You've been pretty quiet, Al," Ben said. "Got any ideas?"

"I'd like to know more about this Burton Catton. She was cheating on him. He took it pretty casual. If Betty ever did that to me, I'd go off like a rocket."

"I know the man," Matthews said. "You wouldn't believe the way he's changed. He used to be the jolly boy type. He had a dreadful harridan of a wife named Ethel. At the time he married her, he was selling insurance and real estate. She was pretty well loaded. She backed him in his first deal. That was a hell of a long time ago. He bought the city dump."

"That sounds just dandy," Spence said.

"It was. The city was abandoning it. It needed a hell of a lot of fill. He was high bidder for it. He'd made arrangements with a contractor who was making that big cut where they rerouted Eastern Avenue. So he got the fill for the cost of hauling it. He got it hauled free by giving a trucker a piece of the pie. They filled it, landscaped it, renamed it, cut it up into approved plots, and just when they were about to start unloading it, the new Vulcan plant was announced. So Burt incorporated, took in a builder, and started putting up houses. They were sold as fast as they could get them up. They were pretty damn shoddy little houses. You know the area. Lakewood Estates it's called. From then on he rolled like a big ball. Belonged to everything. He built that camp as a hideaway, to get away from Ethel. He lived hard and drank hard and chased the women. I was out there twice, at stag picnics he used to have. Free liquor and some pretty gaudy entertainment. Then, last year, when he was riding high, things started to go sour for him. Right when he was at the top. He'd married Drusilla after Ethel died. Big money, a handsome young wife, and a lot of laughs. And he got careless. The Director of Internal Revenue turned that laugh into a sickly smile."

"Fraud?" Ben asked.

"They didn't try to make that stick. They just handed him a fat deficiency judgment. As I understand it, Burt had taken capital gains on a lot of big land deals. So they reclassified him as a land merchant, and made it retroactive several years, so what he had taken as capital gains had to be considered as income. He fought it, but they made it stick. He got hurt badly and so did the people in with him. Most of them could stand it because they'd only had a small piece of his syndicate operations. As I heard it, a lawyer named Verney took a big clouting."

Ben turned and stared at Matthews. For a moment the siren made conversation impossible. When the sound died, Ben said, "Paul Verney?"

"Do you know him?"

"I know him." Spence said "He came into this thing through Johnny Keefler. That's how we found out Danny was trying to plant an envelope somewhere."

Ben felt, deep inside him, that familiar and telltale surge of excitement. "I'm a guy who takes long looks at coincidences, Wendy."

Matthews said, "Let me get this. It was Verney who told Bronson he wouldn't hold onto his envelope for him."

"He told Keefler that Bronson acted so strange he didn't want to get mixed up in it."

"That's what he told me," Spence said.

"How big a man is he?" Ben asked Spence.

"He's a pretty good-sized bastard. He isn't heavy, but he's tall and sort of what you call raw-boned, and he's got a pair of meat hooks on him like that guy that used to like to bust down doors when they had him on the Vice Section. He's about forty. A very solemn type guy. Sits there behind his desk like somebody was engraving his picture to put on a thousand-dollar bill."

"He sold you?" Ben asked.

"No reason why he shouldn't. He talked just fine. Got a nice office. Gave me a hell of a good cigar."

Matthews said, "He has the reputation of being almost too shrewd, Ben. He worked pretty closely with Burt Catton for years."

"Okay," Ben said, "here's a question for you. We'll assume he was hurt bad by the tax decision. We'll take it another step and we'll assume he had figured out some fancy way to make up his losses. How the hell would Drusilla Catton know about it, know enough about it to give Danny a lever to use? Were he and Drusilla playmates?"

"I would doubt that. Verney had a wife in an institution somewhere. And a son away at school. He's never, as far as I know, had much to do with women. I think he would be too heavy-handed for Drusilla."

"Is he in any position of trust where he could be taking the wrong money? Estate work, maybe?"

"I wouldn't think so. At least no important estates."

"The penalty is the same."

"But he couldn't get healthy on a small estate. That was a big tax bill, the way I heard it."

Spence said, "I'll just throw this in and you can kick it around. If Catton and Verney were so close, maybe they got a deal where they can both get healthy. Then maybe Mrs. Catton would have found out from her husband and told Danny."

"Then why not squeeze Catton?" Ben asked.

"Because of the likelihood he would drop dead," Matthews said.

"I don't know if we're getting anywhere," Ben said.

"Maybe we ought to back up a little," Spence said. "Let's say it was Verney. Okay, how does he know about Lucille Bronson?"

Ben thought in silence for a few moments. "From Johnny Keefler? Wait a minute. We're not doing this logically. We're going too fast. If we assume it's Verney, we have to assume that when Bronson went to see him last Thursday, it was part of the squeeze. This stuff about the envelope was fabricated."

"Maybe he went there for a down payment?" Matthews asked.

Ben hit his fist on his thigh. "Hey! Lucille told her husband Danny had only been there once. Catelli found proof he had been there twice. Lucille told her husband Bronson had left the money there way back on September twenty-eighth. The recent prints could have been made last Thursday. Suppose on Danny's first visit, he left the statement of what he'd found out about Verney. He spent a long time figuring out just how he'd handle it. Last Thursday he contacted Verney, got a thousand bucks, left it with Lucille the same day, as an emergency escape fund if the rest of it went sour."

"Why not take it out to the camp?" Matthews asked.

"Maybe Drusilla had the idea she was going to go with him. If he wanted to go alone, it would be wise to stash the money some other place."

"Too many assumptions," Matthews said.

"We can check any withdrawal Verney may have made that day," Ben said.

"He's got a safe in his office," Spencer said. "It could have come out of there."

"As soon as we get back, Al," Ben said, "I want you and Dan Means to concentrate on Paul Verney. Find out what he was doing Tuesday evening and Wednesday morning. I'm going to talk to Johnny Keefler."

"I'll talk to Burt Catton," Matthews said.

Keefler had become a hollow man, a little empty-eyed ghost who talked in a listless and barely audible voice. It took Wixler a long time to bring Keefler around to his remembrance of the talk with Verney, and even longer to isolate the key factor in the conversation.

"Now let's get this straight, Johnny. After Verney told you about the envelope, *then* you and he discussed where Danny could have left it?"

"I guess so."

"What did you say, specifically?"

"—"

"Come on, Johnny. What did you say?"

"I . . . I said if Lee Bronson and his wife had lied to me I was going to give them a hard time."

"Did you say *when* you were going to give them this hard time?"

"I guess I said right away."

"And *then* he suddenly happened to remember those two names?"

"Yes. He forgot them, he said. Then he remembered. He told me. And I checked them out and . . ."

"I can't hear you, Johnny. Talk louder."

"Then you picked me up."

He tried to ask more questions, but Keefler had gone too far away. He did not seem to hear. When Ben shook him by the shoulder there was no resistance, no awareness. The man's lips moved. He looked back after he left the cell. Johnny Keefler sat in a gray huddle on the bunk, good hand clasping the wrist of the mutilated left arm, his shadow made starkly black by the blue-white flare of the recessed fluorescence in the ceiling overhead.

CHAPTER TWELVE

At eight o'clock on Friday evening, Ben Wixler sat waiting. He did not hear Beth tell him the kids were in bed until she spoke the second time. Then he stood up heavily and went in and said good night to them.

They walked back into the living room. He stood by the picture window and looked out at the rainy street under the lights. She came up beside him and touched his arm.

"Bad?" she said softly.

"It's supposed to be good," he said. "It's what they pay me for. Remember me? I'm Ben Wixler, nemesis."

"So bitter, baby."

"It's all so damn stupid. Three of them dead. And two dying. I didn't tell you about that. About Catton. Wendy interrogated him. Catton was fine. Then Wendy worked his way around to the key question. What illegal thing was he doing, in partnership with Paul Verney? Wendy said Catton's mouth worked and nothing came out and he turned the color of spoiled yeast and Wendy caught him as he toppled off the chair. He's in an oxygen tent. He can't talk and we won't talk, and the medical profession is astonished he lasted until this afternoon. He may be gone by now. It stoned Wendy. But it was another confirmation."

"You're certain now?"

"Certain. Verney is the other dying man. He doesn't know it yet. I don't know why he didn't cover himself better. He left it so open he can't prove he wasn't at Lee Bronson's Tuesday night. And he even told his office staff he was out near Kemp on Wednesday morning. I think it's a kind of intellectual arrogance with him. In his own way he may be as crazy as poor Johnny Keefler. He should have known that sooner or later we'd check him.

Even if there was no talk with Keefler, we would have checked him as a matter of routine when we ran out of other answers. And he isn't ready for it. My God, his own secretary was able to tell us he left his office with Danny Bronson Thursday morning. He withdrew one thousand and one hundred dollars in cash. The teller remembers he asked for a thousand in fifties, a hundred in twenties. He thinks he's so damn shrewd. He's a sitting rabbit. We'll blow his head off before he can wiggle."

She gave him a wry smile. "So you prefer your killers to be smarter, darling?"

He smiled back. "Even though he was clumsy, it's a change from the ball peen hammer in the furnished room type deal."

She winced. "Puh-leeze."

The phone rang. He hurried to it.

"Cullin, Sergeant. It's all set. He got in fifteen minutes ago. It's staked out. Dan has the warrant and he's on the way to pick you up, along with Catelli."

Ben put on his raincoat and hat. He kissed Beth. She stood and watched through the picture window as he got into the sedan. She saw it drive away. She felt a great gladness that he was the sort of man he was, able to be depressed by the things he had to do. She hoped the years would never dull that sensitivity. She hoped he could never become callously indifferent to the human beings he trapped.

Lee Bronson arrived back at his rented house at eight-fifteen on Friday night. He had left immediately after the funeral and had driven back through the gray rain to Hancock. He felt emotionally drained. Through all their tears they had looked at him with eyes of stone. He was the betrayer who had taken their lovely child, their only child, to a faraway place and, through his negligence, had permitted her to be slain. They made no attempt to speak to him, nor did any of her childhood friends. He had stood apart from all of them.

When he watched the casket lowered into the October ground it was still unbelievable to him. He remembered

156

how she had reveled in sunlight, how she enjoyed the hot pulse of the sun on her perfect body.

Now he was permitted to return to his home.

She had left an emptiness. When, with the permission of the police, her parents had come to this house to take away her personal belongings, the screaming scene they made had made him wish he could turn and run from them. They had stripped the house of everything that had been hers, and a few things that were not hers, such as the small radio she had given him, and one table lamp that had been in the house when they had rented it. It was not worth a protest.

He walked through the oppressive silence of the house and estimated how long it would take him to pack, how much luggage he would need. His two suitcases and a big crate for the books and papers. That should do it.

When the phone rang, startling him, he let it ring five times before he answered it. He thought it could be a diehard reporter.

"Yes?" he said cautiously.

"Lee. Haughton here. I'm wondering about Monday. Will you take your classes?"

"I . . . don't know."

"The first day will be difficult. But the little animals have short memories."

"I had the idea I might go away for a while, Dr. Haughton."

"I see."

"I don't want to let you down."

"My dear young man, I have been disappointed in the human race my entire life. I will call your attention to two things. One—your sad showing in our chess match. Two—the mute and helpless woe that will be the lot of one Jill Grossman, a highly talented child who can use much guidance."

"Well, I . . ."

"And think of your cretins who may lose invaluable games because you are not there to tell them how to use their clumsy muscles. Show up on Monday, Mr. Bronson. That is an order."

The phone clicked. Lee stood holding the receiver. He replaced it gently on the cradle. And suddenly he smiled.

It was eight thirty-five on Friday evening when Paul Verney heard the footsteps in the hallway and heard the brisk knock on his door. He had been sitting in his deep leather chair ever since he had returned to his room. He had been trying to think his way out of a mood of blackest depression. The body of Bronson had been found too readily. It was ominous that Burt had collapsed while being questioned by the police. He could see how it could all have been managed in other more careful ways. He wished he had not talked to Keefler. He was trying to hearten himself with the idea they had absolutely no proof. None. They could be suspicious, but there could never be any actual proof. The gun and black gloves were buried in a swamp halfway between Kemp and Hancock.

The knock had an official sound that made his heart leap in his chest. He crossed the room and opened the door. There were three men. One of them was Detective Spence, whose confidence had been so dismaying. A bigger man with a wet trench coat and an air of authority said, "Mr. Verney? I'm Sergeant Wixler. You know Detective Spence. And this is Mr. Catelli. I have a warrant here to search this room. Would you care to examine it?"

"A warrant? On what basis, Sergeant?"

"We're looking for evidence, Mr. Verney. I hereby inform you that you are under arrest for suspicion of murder. The murder of Lucille Bronson, Daniel Bronson, and Drusilla Catton."

Verney's mind, racing quickly, decided at once there could be no evidence in this room. It strengthened his response. "You people must be out of your minds."

Detective Spence circled him, searched his person quickly and effectively and said, "Stand over against that wall, Mr. Verney."

"I'll be happy to co-operate in any way I can, but . . ."

"You can talk later," Wixler said.

Verney watched them. The man named Catelli had a small case with him. Catelli went to the closet, opened the closet door and sat on the floor. He opened his case. He took a strong flashlight and began to pick up, one by one, Verney's shoes, taking the left shoe in each case and paying attention to the outside edge of the shoe. Verney began to feel a surprising emptiness in his belly, pangs like those of hunger.

Catelli gave a grunt of satisfaction. He was holding a black shoe, examining it closely under the light. Verney knew he had worn that pair when he had gone to 1024 Arcadia Street. He tried to tell himself this was some sort of a trick, but there was a curious roaring sound in his ears.

"Got it?" Wixler asked.

"I think so." Catelli was a wiry man with a satanic grin. The light cast its beams upward onto his face. He said, "How about it, Sarge? A lot of people who don't know how this is done get a boot out of it. Maybe Mr. Verney wants to see better, hey?"

Wixler nodded and stepped to one side. Spence urged Verney closer.

Catelli looked very pleased. "This is one of the things you got to know how to do in my business." He took a small square of paper, white and flimsy. "Now this here is filter paper. In this bottle here I got a one-tenth-N-saline solution. I get this here paper nice and moist. Then, see, I press it against this little stain here on the edge of the sole of your shoe. Okay. From here on I don't need the shoe. In this here bottle a two hundred and forty-to-one solution of Eastman 3620 in acetic acid at forty per cent strength. So I take this glass rod and dip it in this bottle and touch it to the filter paper where I pressed it against the shoe. Check? Nothing happens yet, Mr. Verney. Not until we get to this last bottle. In this bottle I got a mixture of eleven parts sodium perborate to thirty parts of a forty per cent acetic acid solution.

"So I wipe off this here rod and dip it in this bottle." He held it over the filter paper. "Now if that spot you had on your shoe was human blood, Mr. Verney, you're going to see this paper change color when I touch it. It'll change to a nice kinda greeny blue, and there isn't another damn thing in the world but blood that'll make it change."

With a certain ceremonial grace, Catelli touched the wet

rod to the paper. The blue-green stain appeared immediately, and Catelli held it up proudly for Verney to see. "So maybe you cut yourself shaving, or maybe you walked where a pedestrian got clobbered. It ain't my business how you got it. All I know is it's blood and it was on your shoe."

Verney stared at the piece of paper. He could feel the other two watching him closely. He knew he had to say something. He took in a deep breath and let it out. He knew he had to explain quickly and logically. He could think of nothing. Yet he had to think of something. He kept staring at the blue-green stain. He sucked in another deep breath. And exploded it out of his lungs in a high whistling, whinnying scream, a shocking scream of fright and despair.

He staggered Spence with a backhand flail of his arm that caught Spence across the chest. He kicked at the paper and missed. Wixler moved trimly, compactly, and with a half swing laid the side of his service revolver over Verney's ear.

Verney fell heavily and lay still.

"The poor son of a bitch," Spence said.

"Pack up, Catelli," Ben said.